# WILLOW'S FLAME

**Do You Really Know Who You're Sleeping Next To?**

## STEPHANIE FIELDS

Dear Jern,

Enjoy the thriller ride.
You might need a Pauleen
pill after. :)

Happy reading!

Stephanie Fields

Published by Pen It! Publications, LLC in the U.S.A.
812-371-4128    www.penitpublications.com

ISBN: 978-1-63984-063-2
Edited by Dina Husseini
Cover Design by Donna Cook

# Table of Contents

# Present Day

The end. No, seriously, this is the end.

It only makes sense to start at the end because beginnings lead to it, anyway. So, I'll give you what you're looking for right up front.

It is a clear, starless black night. A cold breeze sets in, making the hair on my skin stand. My frizzy curls dance, smacking my face every thirty seconds. I keep my hands still, placed on my lap.

*I deserved to be slapped across the face.*

My eyes water with the sting of the crisp night air. The bottom sides of the bucket I sit on top of dig into the back of my thighs, leaving marks deep and blood red. I stay seated on top of that bucket for hours, feeling lethargic and finally being able to catch my breath. The deeper it digs into my backside, the more numb I feel. I let it do its job. I let it stab me so hard that it numbs all of me from the inside out.

*Finally.*

When the numbness consumes me, I reject it. I stand and kick the bucket across the field, hard. I let out a scream I know no one can hear. Dropping down on the cold wet grass, I feel it ease up the indentions on the back of my bare legs. I inhale a big gasp and hold it in as I swing my body to fall flat onto the ground, letting the earth become my bed to cry on. The tears well from deep inside and course down my cheeks. I let out a moan and howl that would haunt a mother's nightmares with the thought of her daughter needing her; shattering every bit of her broken heart.

*My baby cried for me.*

I yank out my "luscious locks" everyone just loves so much and pinch my arms black and blue until I become lethargic once more. I curl into a ball, hugging myself I suppose to comfort, not that I deserve that because I am a murderer. I did kill someone.

People who take another person's life just don't deserve to be patted on the back afterwards. No. I don't deserve this hug.

*You made your bed, now lie in it,* my mother would say.

And so, I do. I stay right there on the cold and wet ground all night and even for a few days after, not even caring that I hadn't eaten a bite of food or had a drop of water touch my tongue. My mouth is dry and cracking and peeling.

Someone out there does care, though. My body is stumbled upon, and I can just faintly hear a man and a woman talking to each other. Their voices get closer and closer to me. They think I'm a victim of some brutal attack with the bruises from my pinching tattooed into sleeves on my arms, my hair is matted and mangled with leaves making their home in between the tresses. My black floral sundress is smeared of mud and grass stains and blood. My dirty bare feet show, and my shoes are nowhere to be found.

The couple feels sorry for me, as any normal person should. They each grab a hold of me and hoist my dead weight of a body up off the ground. They walk me to their car. They're talking to me, but I can't make out what they say. The day is too loud and bright. When we get to their car, they gently lay my frail body in the back seat. I smell cleanliness and a cheap car freshener in the air. The stains I'll leave behind on their pearl white seats will tell a sad story indeed.

"What's your name?" the woman asks. But I don't answer her. I'm not trying to be rebellious against them, like a child who refuses to answer their parents or teachers questions. I stay quiet, though. I'm just freezing and starving and weak.

"Can you hear me?" she tries again.

"Willow" I whisper and my throat hurts. It feels and tastes like blood back there.

"Willow. That's a pretty name. Can you tell me who did this to you, Willow?" Her voice sounds like a teacher's does when they're getting down to the bottom of who started it on the playground.

*Me. I did this.*

But again, I say nothing. And this time I really say nothing. I press and hold my lips together, close my eyes and fall asleep because that's all my weak body can do.

I'm awakened by a needle piercing into a vein in my arm. I lay there lifeless, letting the doctors and nurses poke and prod at me however they like. They sedate me with enough morphine to kill off all the physical and mental pain I feel. I'm loopy-headed and feeling pretty damn good as I sing out loud Ironic, by Alanis Morissete.

2

My off-tune singing continues while they roll me from triage to the recovery room. I'm having the time of my life, and as I look up, I'm met with a few faces covered in hospital masks peering down at me. The wrinkles that surround their eyes show me they're smiling at me. They think I'm funny. I think they like the way I sing. Those faces are the last of what I see before falling back asleep.

When I wake up, I notice fresh flowers on the window seal of the room I'm recovering in. The couple who saved my life are gone, but they left me a card and a balloon with get well soon in bright colors marked on both. The bouquet is from all the staff. It's not a cheap one, either. The assortment is beautifully put together. Those dainty multi-colored flowers have already blossomed and bloomed. I open the card from the couple and read the note they left for me. It was just a simple little quote on the inside, and they wrote that they'll be back to check on me.

They signed it with *Mr. & Mrs. Grey*.

A petite, bubbly nurse walks in with a plate of hospital food balanced on a tray and when she sets it in front of me, I devour it all within minutes, starting with the Jell-O. The red, strawberry kind. My favorite.

She stays to witness the starved prisoner finally getting to eat, and I feel awkward scarfing my food down in front of her. Every single crumb vanishes off the plate as she stands there to watch me eat. I eyeball her a few times, hoping she doesn't take it away before I can finish it. She smiles and tells me there's more where that came from, before walking back into the hospital halls to a few nurses that peer into the room I lay in. They whisper to each other as they walk away. I don't hear what they're saying, but I can only imagine.

I know what they're all thinking; I'm a victim of some psychosexual predator and he's out on the loose, stalking his next prey. The next beautiful innocent young woman who's just headed home from the pub or library or grocery store will be unfortunate.

*Boy, are they ever so wrong!*

I'm a cold-blooded killer, but I'm not ready to admit such a thing just yet, because now that I'm thinking clearly, I remember why I did it. But I wonder…

*How many lives do you have to take before you're labeled a serial killer?*

# One Year Ago
## Neil & Willow

Willow glared down at her phone, smiling the way she used to when she'd get a funny text sent by me from across the room. It seemed like our humor was made for each other. I could remember when my jokes made her laugh so much that she'd let out a little snort or run to the bathroom hardly being able to contain her laughter, yelling out she's about to wet herself.

It seemed like a lifetime ago that we connected that way. In any way really. When she's knocked out from the pill I crushed up and put in her ritual nighttime drink, I would go through her phone. The only thing that kept her undivided attention at the time. It would only be then that I'd know what had got her blushing those raspberry rosy cheeks because sadly, it sure as hell wasn't me. I wasn't going to succumb to this, but she was so distant, and I had to figure her out somehow.

Besides, it was just half a Xanax.

I bought a few off my neighbor, Pauleen. Willow and I usually avoided any eye contact with her at all costs. Eye contact meant the longest five minutes of my life listening to her talk about her arthritis pain and the extreme anxiety she deals with due to all the medical issues she has. This is how I knew she had plenty of pain and anxiety pills to go around the block a time or two. Even just a five-minute little conversation *that felt like an eternity*, she told us too much about her boring life all hopped up on pills.

*Blah blah blah. We get it, Pauleen. You're old. Can I have my pills now? Thanks.*

Listening to nosey, talkative neighbors paid off in the end. I told her not to mention anything about it to Willow and paid her a little extra to keep quiet, because ya know... *that'll give me even more anxiety.* I

5

had to know what or *who* had caused mine and Willow's unannounced separation. It was eating at my very core. Swallowing me whole until I was indefinitely invisible to her.

***

"I haven't slept that hard in ages." Willow yawned the next morning, sleepy eyed and spreading cream cheese on a bagel. She sat at the breakfast nook with her phone faced down.

*Of course, it's faced down. It's always faced down.*

I didn't find a thing in her vice. Nothing. Nadda. Zilch. I didn't even find anything funny; nothing exactly worth laughing at. So, what made her smile that way? I did, however, take note of her schedule. Something she started to avoid telling me like the plague.

Some people might have judged me for planning to spy on her. They probably would have even call it stalking. But it's not spying and it's not stalking, because she was my wife.

*I owned her.*

Anyway, I wouldn't have had to do this if she would have just told me what was wrong. We got hitched three years ago and I hadn't done anything like this before. That counts for something.

Doesn't it? And that's how I knew I'm not the bad guy here. She was.

***

I snuck up behind her as she gazed at her reflection, both hands held up those soft spiral curls I loved so much, exposing the little mole on her neck. She called it her beauty mark. I placed my lips where in the past would have halted her movements and she'd give herself to me.

Once upon a time this would have driven her wild, made her late for work. But instead, she pulled back from me. Making the excuse she's running behind, when in fact she would be early leaving half an hour from the time it was.

Rushing out the door she doesn't say bye, good day, fuck off. She just left me behind like I was some roommate she's tired of sharing a hallway with.

That day I didn't follow her. I let her do what she wanted. This was my test. A way of seeing what decisions she'd make and what time she'd come home. I'd take note if her hair was scuffled, or her blouse was sideways when she got here. She got done with work at three o' clock and had a fifteen-minute commute. I'd give her the other fifteen to stop and smell the flowers.

If she wasn't home by four, I'd know she's up to no good.

Having pictures of her schedule for the next few months on my phone was enough to satisfy me for the time being.

Besides, I had work of my own to do.

***

A pile of dusty, stacked up folders leaned sideways, begging for his attention. Boring tasks left for him to complete. Larger than life numbers gleamed at him, waiting to be cleaned up of their owner's faults. He had been a little excited about getting the financial advisor job handed to him straight out of Junior College. He had thought he'd move up the chain by now, become someone important. He had liked the job at first because it was easy for him. He was a smart guy, after all. But he began to loath it.

*A pointless job that ultimately fills someone else's pocket* is a way he'd describe it to Willow when she'd ask how work was going. She didn't ask him that question anymore.

Neil knew he was too good for such insignificance anyway. So, he left those folders closed and let them pile up dust a little longer. Instead of working for other people, he got hard at work on something for himself. He opened a browser on the computer and typed in *Ways to know your wife is cheating on you*. Reading one article after another, he enabled the online world to unfold before his very eyes the secrets Willow had been keeping. Steam rose to his cheeks as he learned that according to everyone who writes articles online about cheating, his wife is most certainly a fucking cheater.

He watched the grandfather clock Willow loved so much tick to 4:03. Anger seeped through his veins and his jaw clenched.

*"I swear if she doesn't walk through that door in five fucking minutes I'm out. And I will find her!"* He yelled loudly, standing from the desk and pacing the floors of his mediocre home office. His fists tightened,

ready to make his way to catch his wife in the act and beat the living shit out of the asshole taking advantage of her.

She walked through the front door and the blood rushing through him turned cold. All of her junk from the day piled the entry way table, freeing her hands that he wanted to grab a hold of. He greeted her in the entrance, wearing a forced smile. She in turn gave him a half smile.

"Long day?" He stood with both hands in his front pockets.

"My boss is the worst." she complained.

"Wanna talk about it?" Trying to make small talk with this woman who used to share everything with him.

In the not so long ago-past, they would share every little detail of their day to each other. She'd text him while at work, and he even knew her coworkers by name. They'd laugh together and gossip about all the drama happening throughout her day.

She opened her mouth like she was about to give in and looked into his eyes. He got lost in hers.

"No," she said.

She pushed past him, and the heat rose to his cheeks once again.

***

I was tired of this emotional roller coaster she'd been forcing me to ride. But, you see, I had secrets also. I didn't show her my anger *(that much)*. I didn't tell her I knew she's a lying ass cheater. And I didn't tell her I had her schedule. My suspicions were kept inside. Sure, they devoured my every waking moment. I'm only human.

But I was smart. I was savvy. I was cool and resilient. I was calm and collective. She was not any of those things. She was messy and clumsy. Her secret wouldn't be hidden much longer. She had never known how to keep one. She was too emotional to hold something so big inside. She'd need the drama of her friends looking at her with wide eyes.

*"So, how big is it?"* Anna would ask. I could just picture Willow laughing and playfully pushing against her shoulder telling her to stop, as she draws out the oh sound with a whiny voice. Listening to her fantasies of who she thought was better than me, and they'd gossip about our life together.

*Or lack of.* It would slip. And when it did, I would have won. It would get around without a doubt, and she'd look like the bad guy to all her family and friends.

*Because she was.*

And they'd all talk her into staying with me because I was good for her. Because I'd forgive her.

She would in turn be at my mercy for life.

*** 

When I lay down beside Willow at night, she would roll to face away from me. I had studied her backside so much that I logged silly little things. Like her hair could use a trimming and her favorite bedtime t-shirt had a bleach stain on the back of it. I didn't tell her. I didn't ruin it for her.

Because all I wanted was for her to be happy. We used to kiss each other goodnight before we fell asleep. *Always kiss me goodnight. Cliche', I know.* It honestly meant everything to me, and then it had become this empty feeling.

The emptiness tightened up around me as a car honking its horn blared outside, and the streetlights peeked into our bedroom windows. The city was alive. *I should have bought that damn blackout curtain.* But then I wouldn't have gotten to take in her silhouette and drink from the curves of her body when she got too hot and tossed the covers off.

I slid my hand up her smooth creamy thigh and she lays there, still. Still as a statue. I knew she was awake because she was just moving. When my hand slid to her front, she quickly grabbed it.

"I don't feel good." she reminded me, tapping my hand. And I didn't miss my cue. I put my hand back on my side of the bed. Like the good little bitch that I was.

*It would soon be her turn, though.*

***

Beads of sweat dripped down my forehead. I fanned my face and Willow copied me to show that I'm not alone.

"It's hot," I spouted the obvious.

"Yeah," she said, laughing for no reason other than the liquor kicking in.

The bar had a cover charge for a band on stage called *The Vikings*. Indie musicians always welcome a good first date ice breaker.

"It's loud." I yelled from across the table. "Do you wanna go somewhere else? Somewhere we can talk?"

"Yeah," she said that one word again. *Yeah.*

Those four little letters jumbled together were the beginning of us. By the end of the night, I just knew we were going to last.

\*\*\*

Panic crawled through my body and reached to my throat. Two doors stood closed, waiting for my bride to delicately glide through.

*What if she changed her mind? What if she decided she likes someone else better than me, and she's standing me up? What if she found out that I—*

The doors swung open and my Goddess ventured through, searching the courtroom for me. She was wrapped in white lace; a form-fitted short dress showing her fit, smooth legs and just how curvy her body was shaped like an hourglass. Her gown was simplistic to match what type of gal she was. She didn't want a big shindig. She even said our marriage wouldn't have all those people in it, so our wedding shouldn't either.

"It's just you and me together against this big fat world," she pawed at me, clamping her hand in mine. She looked into my eyes, swaying along to Eric Clapton as he sang about just how *wonderful* she looks tonight. And her body pressed against mine, she smiled and bit her lip a little at me. That was the second-best day of my life. Because on this day I married her. The day I got to finally call her mine.

\*\*\*

Three years. Only three short years I had Willow by my side. And if you're not counting the number of times she had dismissed me, *which I don't*, well then, it's only been two years.

That's 730 days I got to taste her soft lips, hold her at night until she fell asleep, feel her body without her recoiling from my touch, look long enough into her eyes to see her face turn pink and then look down, then back up at me with that perfect smile of hers.

When we got married, I told her she didn't need to work anymore. My job paid enough for the place we stayed. Our apartment was a cheap, small one bedroom, one bath right smack dab in the middle of Chicago.

Once upon a time the building was white from the view of the streets, but now it's faded into a piss yellow color from the neglect, and leafy vines crawl up the sides like spiders.

But living there was convenient for us. There was plenty of shopping and dining within walking distance. Our parents wanted us to move to Naperville. Just outside of Chicago, but much nicer on the eyes and safer to live. Which also meant it was much more expensive. We decided on the city, to be surrounded by art and opportunities.

*And* so, we wouldn't go broke just trying to live. We liked it there.

Home was wherever she was, anyway. We didn't need a big fancy house to show off. We only needed each other. I'd live in a box as long as she was with me.

She declined my suggestion of quitting her job. I let it slide because she really did love her job. She called it a *career*. I didn't tell her that working as a journalist is just a job.

A career is stable and she was far from that. She made little to nothing. A *career* would be if she was successful, but she was considered a peon to everyone up there she worked alongside in her cubicle. She was just too blind to see it. With big aspirations she clocked in at her thirty-hour unstable scheduled work week *job* and gave it her all.

She poured more of herself into *that* than she did to me. They didn't appreciate her there. And she didn't appreciate *me* for giving her the option to be a housewife. She could have stayed at home with me; my office was there. She could have cooked us lunch every day. We could have enjoyed each other's company during my break, but instead I ate cold ravioli out of a can.

\*\*\*

Stomping around the apartment, Willow threw a fit, "Why the fuck is it you can't or *won't* pick up after yourself?" She picked up a pair of crusty, dirty rolled up socks Neil took off earlier that day. She didn't understand how his socks got so filthy like this. He worked from home.

*What the hell was he doing?*

11

"Come on now, honey." Neil calmly said to her. "Sit down and watch some T.V. with me. Our show is on." He sat on the couch; one leg tossed over the other.

For the longest time they would bond by snuggling on the couch together with a pile of soft Autumn colored decorative pillows surrounding them, and they'd watch Netflix shows. Willow wouldn't move onto the next episode without Neil, and he'd do the same for her. This night, Neil had put on *Dead to Me*.

She took a deep breath and let it all out, "Okay. You're right. These things can be done later."

"Exactly. You can clean tomorrow after work." Neil kept his eyes glued on the television.

Willow stopped in her tracks and gave him a death glare. "Are you suggesting that *I* clean everything? Why wouldn't you say *we* can clean tomorrow after work?"

"Welcome to marriage, darling." He showed that devious smile she used to like. In the past she thought of that smile to be playful and forgiving, but here lately she had noticed it was actually a dark part of his character. The part she didn't like about him. He'd give that smile when he meant exactly what he said, whether what he had just said was something shitty or not.

When Neil knew he tricked you into whatever it was he finally got from you, that's when he'd give that devious smile.

The glass of cola in his hand clinked ice together as he took a drink. Then he sat it back down on the coffee table and continued watching the show.

And it was then that Willow began to question their marriage for the second time.

*** 

Willow would have done just about anything to get out of spending time with me. She met up with her friends once a week for drinks but didn't ever invite me anymore. Her friends were less than impressive anyway. Anna was promiscuous, and Willow was impressionable like a child. I got worried she'd follow into her footsteps and lead to temptation.

Bridget was a bitch. She talked about Willow behind her back, but my darling wife only vented to me about it because God forbid her confront the Queen B of the group. And then there's Stacey. She was nice enough, but only to get her way. Some people call that manipulation. I do too. So, even if Willow *did* invite me out with her friends I may have actually said no anyway.

But hey, it's the thought that counts, right?

In the past she would meet me on her lunch break, and we'd dine at a little sandwich shop down the road from her office. But now she had stopped opening my text when I'd invite her to eat. She left me on unread, time and time again. No little green check mark appeared beside the messages I sent her anymore. She must have had a few hundred unread texts from me by now, just sitting idle.

What happened to us?

She was spending a lot of time lately with new people she met at some stupid book club she tried getting me to tag along with her to. She ranted and raved about, *The, oh so, amazing Branded Book Club* and couldn't wait to start reading with people who *actually like to read* she'd say.

As if reading was the most important thing of all. I, however, always thought she joined *just* to be able to meet new people. She was a social butterfly and needed mounds and mounds of attention from strangers. I'd rather be at home, though. I tried to talk her out of going, but she persisted with puppy dog eyes and got her way.

*Being nice to get what you want.*

I was fine with her going, after all it was only once a month for just a few hours. But then, she met *him*.

And, I knew their friendship would tear us apart.

*** 

"You have problems. You're crazy!" Willow spat as she yanked down the bottle of laundry soap off the shelf in the laundry room. Liquid splashed on her cheek, and she wiped it off angrily, leaving a blue smudge on her face from the detergent.

"Listen. All I'm saying is you can find other friends. He's not your *friend*, Willow. He wants to be more than that." I tried explaining to her.

"And you would know this how?" she questioned me like I was just born yesterday.

"Because I'm a guy."

"Oh. Classic." She rolled her eyes, then she gave a little laugh and shook her head in disbelief. "Just wow!"

"No. I didn't mean it like that," pleading for her to understand me.

Placing her hands on her hips, she interrogated me "Then how *did* you mean it, Neil?"

I sighed and hung my head. *Why wouldn't she do what I say?*

"You're just jealous and insecure." And the words stabbed right through me.

\*\*\*

Neil's eyes darted daggers at Willow right then. He clenched his jaw and she could see this. She pointed her eyes down. Not wanting to see again what kind of darkness she noticed glimmer in them. Shifting one foot then the other.

"Can I get by?" she asked.

He elevated his arm out with an open hand and bowed his head downward. The pounding heart in her chest felt like it would eventually beat through. She slowly walked past him and let out a skittish whisper, "Thank you."

Because for some reason she felt like she needed to act grateful for a simple, small gesture that wouldn't normally need to be thanked. She couldn't quite put a finger on it, but she knew she felt uneasy. It was the look in Neil's eyes that had scared her.

She felt goose bumps covering her arms, legs and the back of her neck. She knew that if she said she was nervous just because of a look he gave her, she'd sound utterly ridiculous. She really didn't know what to say or think, but she did know what she felt. She felt uneasy. She saw a hint of dark threats reflecting in his eyes. She rolled the charm on her necklace back and forth against her chin nervously and told him what he wanted to hear.

"Okay. I won't talk to him anymore."

# Brock

Working a factory job was 50/50 for Brock. He enjoyed the labor. It made him sweat the toxins out that he needed to get rid of. It gave him purpose and helped him to feel like a man. But he hated the people he worked with.

Pallets of wood lay in rows ahead of him, waiting for their limbs to be sawed off and repurposed into furniture for people to enjoy. His phone rang at him and lit up; a notification he was excited to open. He'd been waiting for this text all day. He knew Willow had to be the first one to text.

*This made me think of you,*

It was a picture of a seductive mouth whispering in a man's ear and read: *"Do that thing I like,"* and underneath showed a man on the phone ordering a large pepperoni pizza.

He ran his hands through his thick dark hair, smiled with his lips together and his head tipping down slightly.

He replied, *"And we love it",* then began a search for a funny meme to send back to her.

The day manager reminded him to get back to work.

"We don't have time for games around here, son. You can chat with your little girlfriend later."

And he winced at the disgust he normally felt when he heard that man's voice.

\*\*\*

"Hey. Leave some for me, big chiefer," Willow teased.

"I got plenty. We won't run out" Brock said after he inhaled.

Uncontrollable coughing dispensed from his body, and they laughed with their heads laying close together on the roof of his car. The steel was cold against their bodies, but they were too stoned to

15

even notice. As their laughter faded, Willow disturbed him with something he dreaded ever having to hear her say. He knew this day would come sometime, though. He braced for it and held his breath when she said she had to talk to him about something important.

"I told my husband I won't be talking to you anymore," piercing his heart.

"Oh?" passing the joint back to her. "Why's that?"

"Because he *suspects* there may be something more going on. I told him he's crazy." she laughed, waving her hands out to express such ridiculousness.

He let out a sigh, sat up and hugged his knees to his chests. He gazed at the starless sky, trying to ignore what she had just said. If he just didn't respond, maybe it wouldn't be real. She fumbled a little using her elbows to help her up.

Sitting up beside him she playfully shoved her shoulder against his. He didn't look at her face. He couldn't bear to. He instead kept his eyes peeled on a bug crawling on the ground and his high brought his thoughts to the seasons changing.

*Summer was approaching.*

"Maybe it's best to just keep it at the book club. Ya know? Book buddies." she suggested.

"So, we can't text? You have that app we use that disappears after it's read." Brock said, hardly being able to keep the annoyance out of his voice.

"Hey. We got to hang out tonight and smoke together. At least we got to do that before…" She let the words trail off, trying to make him *and herself* feel better about all of this.

She wanted to be good to her husband, but she enjoyed the friendship she had with Brock. And truth be told, she started to feel a little crush coming on.

*Yeah, my bud,* he thought to himself. "Yeah. No. I get it." he said, crinkled his lips and hopped off the car to take her back to hers.

\*\*\*

Willow hadn't posted on Instagram in three days. This wasn't like her. I kept refreshing her page and each time it was the same quote she shared during her last log in.

*"It's better to have loved and lost, than to have never loved at all."*

16

Could this be about me? I wondered if she was alright. The temptation to text her was unbearable. It crawled all over me like little insects by the millions that I couldn't see, but could feel every leg move as it stung my skin, tickled my hair, bit through to my bones. I pulled up her message box and started typing, then backspaced and left her alone.

*Chicken shit.* I had done that so many times now.

***

The room was painted with people of all sizes and colors. Men and women from ages early twenties to seventies made small talk and sipped their fruit punch out of plastic cups with their names written in black sharpie. Smiles plastered their faces. Some drew on fake smiles and filled their cheeks up with air to release all the mundane conversation they just had, as they finally got to walk away from the forced niceties.

Some wore real smiles, bonding with like-minded souls. When the leader walked in, everyone separated to take a seat, and it wasn't so crowded like the other ones I had been to before. There were rows upon rows of blue metal chairs facing the stage, and everyone actually had elbow space.

"Attention ladies and gents. Thank you for joining us. It's only our second night here together with you lovely people and *wow*, what a turn out!" the lady in charge announced.

She wore a red pant suit and resembled Oprah Winfrey more than Oprah Winfrey herself. How is that possible?

Crying and growling shrieks echoed from the back and made its way around the room, violating all of our ears.

"I'm sorry to inform you, but it's in the rules. No children are allowed. Nobody under twenty-one is allowed," the lady in charge reminded the crowd.

The baby's yelping faded as the sullen mother with a messy bun and fresh face drifted away from the adult interaction she craved.

"Welcome to The Branded Book Club!" the lady in charge continued.

Hands clapping together roared through the building.

"Tonight, we embark on a journey different from any other book club around. We're tired of having to go to book clubs with only one

17

book to be *forced* to choose. *Or,* having to go to our local library and *hope* they're showing a book we even want. No more of that. We have all the genres right here in one room. Each genre has a book assigned and we'll rotate to another once all participants finish."

She gazed around the gigantic auditorium and waited for her followers to clap. They did, and she gave a little bow and smiled a bright, white smile.

"So, without further ado, find a book that peaks, *your* interest and introduce yourself to other members of that club. The journey through the minds of *your* choice begins tonight. Let's do this! Let's have some fun!" She preached to all the anxious readers.

She wore an expression you could tell this was the highlight of her life. Her big moment was here. More clapping and howling and loud whistles rang in my ears, and our leader thanked her audience *endlessly.*

I took a walk through the auditorium, gauging reactions from each club. Books of cartoon anime peered at me with big, sad eyes. People dressed as furies slid to the middle of a circle they made, taking their turn of drama for their onlookers. Self-help books yelled at me to *be better* as their readers gathered together to counsel one another.

"It's just been so hard." an overweight, redhead woman's chin quivered, sobbing as the group consoled her.

Fantasy demanded my attention with books of bold colors and their escape world of witches, dragons, the princess and her knight in shining armor. They argued over which is better, *Lord of the Rings* or *Harry Potter?* They excited themselves by the talk of cosplay and action.

I drifted to the thrillers genre and felt at home because the mystery wrapped itself around me like a blanket, I couldn't stand the thought of letting go of. The comfort of suspense. I had drowned in it my whole life.

And then I saw her, showing those straight snow white teeth by laughing genuinely with a fellow thrill seeker.

She wore a sheer-ish floral dress, Hercules sandals and her face was natural with little freckles making a line on her nose and spreading some to her cheeks. Like the ones girls nowadays were purposely drawing on their faces. Hers were natural though, and she wasn't wearing much makeup. Maybe just a touch of mascara and lip gloss, but I could see who she was underneath the color.

*And, my God she was beautiful.*

Her hair was held together by chopsticks for aesthetic, and strands of her loose blonde curls fell just at her almond shaped brown eyes. She noticed me staring and so I quickly grabbed a book and turned it over to read the blurb on the back. I did a double take because she was then walking my way.

*Don't be a pussy. Talk to her.*

She walked straight up to me and introduced herself. Her mouth moved in slow motion to me as she worded the name Willow.

*Willow... What a lovely name.*

"Um. Hi? Hello?" giggling, she waved a hand at me. Shy girl. I dig it. Wedding ring on her finger, not so much.

*Shit. I had been staring again. Just fucking staring at her, not saying a damn thing. Idiot.*

"Hey there," I managed to get out, scratching the back of my head.

She reached her hand out to shake mine and her purse trickled down. She followed and fixed it. She forgot to feel my sweaty palm.

*Thank God.*

"I love the main character of this book, like Dr. Jekyll and Mr. Hyde." She picked up the book and studied the cover. "I've even seen the movie. It's practically the same as the book."

Gillian Flynn, Gone Girl.

"Hey, hey, hey. No spoilers. I haven't read it yet." I played, trying for a flirt. I was never good at flirting. I slid up behind her to look at the book over her shoulder. I knew I could read the one in my hand, but I wanted to get closer to her. She smelled like vanilla.

And, I liked it.

"I wouldn't dream of it. You're gonna *die*. You're gonna *love* it." she beamed at me.

"And, may I ask why you're reading it again when you already know the ending?" I took a step closer to her. We were close enough to kiss.

"Because it's that damn good," shooting me a shy smile, then she licked those delicious pink lips.

# Willow

Sometimes I would catch Neil gazing in my direction with a look of repugnance, like I left a nasty taste in his mouth after taking a bite out of moldy cheesecake. And sometimes he would look at me with satisfaction, like the lion who's been lurking and finally caught his prey. Most of the time his face reflected desperation; I knew it's because I'd been pulling away from him.

His black eyes used to hypnotize me. They'd draw me deep into his world I thought to be one we shared. They started to haunt me in every direction I looked *and didn't look*. Trying to find my way out of this darkness, digging my hands in the earth to crawl out of this hole he's thrown me in to rot and I couldn't; he wouldn't allow it.

It wasn't long after we got married that the fighting began. He immediately wanted to start a family.

*** 

"I mean, I really want two kids; a boy comes first as a bodyguard and then we can have a little girl." Neil came out with it.

"And, I told you before we got married that having kids will never be an option for me and I *thought* you understood that." She reminded him.

"But you *can* have kids, though. Like, your body *works*. You just don't want to put in the *work*." Neil tried for an insult.

"Actually, you're damn right I don't wanna put in the work. We've already discussed this. My body, my choice." She stated for what seemed like the millionth time in her life.

She hated that old school thinking of every woman should bear children, that you're selfish if you don't. She heard enough of that talk from her mom.

"You're my only child and I get no grand babies out of you? That means I get none at all. It's time to grow up and think of someone other than yourself, Willow." her mom griped at her the night of her wedding rehearsal dinner.

The rehearsal dinner wasn't even necessary. They were getting married at the courthouse. But she caved in when her mom told her she wanted to feel like it was a *real wedding*.

And then she started to hear it from Neil. What bothered her the most was he *knew* her life wouldn't ever be of endless chores to another human being, and that's exactly what having a baby would be like to her.

He *knew* she didn't want to bring children into this *God forsaken world*. She told him as much before they got married. But he admitted he faked that approval to keep her.

"Why are you now changing your mind about kids? We've only been home from our honeymoon a week now. Am I just not enough for you?" Willow asked as she unpacked the luggage she left sitting in a corner of their bedroom when they got back from their honeymoon a week before.

"I've always wanted kids," he admitted.

"And you're just now telling me this, why?" She raised her eyebrows at him.

"Because I knew you wouldn't marry me if I told you before."

"Neil, that's conniving. You can't just trick people into marrying you like that." She made direct eye contact with him then.

"Looks like I did." he said quickly with a smirk on his face, propped on their bed with his legs crossed, glaring at her with those dark glazed over eyes.

His velvety, dirty blonde hair stood like a perm. His wardrobe consisted of black or khaki slacks, and every color of button up polo shirts you could imagine. He'd wear the same tennis shoes daily. Neil considered himself a 'minimalist', but really it was just that he couldn't financially afford more than what he had on his back.

She analyzed his posture and listened to the words he just mouthed with that foreign accent to die for.

*A red flag*, she thought.

This was the first time she questioned their marriage. They had only been married a few weeks, and she was already feeling regretful of it. She had never been married before Neil. And she thought perhaps this was just part of getting to know your spouse. All be it; this was a pretty big surprise to throw her way.

She wanted to press and question him further, but she said nothing. And nothing is what she would say to him most of the time after that conversation. Nothing is what became of how she eventually would feel about him. The more she uncovered, the more steps she took back. And that nothing she felt right after their honeymoon consumed her completely in his presence.

\*\*\*

Our first date was a bit of a blur, I admit. I always get drunk on the first date. I don't *mean* to. I simply start off with a shot to loosen up a little. And the next thing I know I've chased a good time with drinks instead of company, and have let it kind of just take over. I don't get sloppy drunk, but I generally end up feeling pretty damn good by the end of the night.

One thing I remember for sure is how easy it was to talk to Neil. And it wasn't just the alcohol kicking in. Our conversation just flowed all evening. His foreign accent seduced me. His devious smile made me feel giddy inside. I'd get butterflies knowing he was on his way to pick me up for a date. When he'd study my eyes, I could feel myself blushing.

It wasn't long after that fuzzy night, that we said, *"I do."*

He proposed to me only four months later. I said yes because I was put on the spot in front of all my friends and family, and I didn't want to embarrass him by telling him how I really felt; that it was just too soon.

But as time went by while we planned the big day, I got to witness the gentleness of his nature towards me, his acceptance of my insane parents, his forgiving of my forgetfulness and clumsiness. These are things about myself that I had always felt insecure about.

I kept my yes answer and pretty soon we were having a Justice of the Peace Wedding. That was the happiest day of my life, I thought at the time. One of them, anyway.

\*\*\*

"Pleeeeease come with me. I *really* think you'll have fun." Willow stood in the entry of Neil's home office.

"Gonna take a rain check on that one, honey." He clicked a pen a few times and read what was on his computer screen.

"You're seriously missing out, though." She pouted her lips and gave a flirty look, thinking sex might work in her favor with this. But he didn't look up from the computer screen to notice her efforts. So, she sulked and listened to the answer she knew he'd give. Once Neil said no about something, he didn't turn back.

"Maybe I'll go to the next meeting. Actually, why don't we both wait for the next one." still keeping his eyes fixated on the computer screen.

"Neil. No. I'm going to this one with or without you. They only happen once a month and this is the one where we choose our book. You can't just join right in the middle of the read. We'll be sharing each month. So, you'll have to start reading... like tomorrow." She held up the flyer of information.

"Then I guess I'll wait for the next book." He snapped at her with barred teeth. He took off his reading glasses and rubbed his eyes, looked at her blankly, then shot her a sarcastic smile.

"Suit yourself, fucking jerk," snapping back at him, she left to head out and let the front door slam behind her.

He jumped when the bang of the screen door slammed closed. Neil stood from his desk and made his way into the kitchen, picking up the flyer he noticed on the floor Willow threw on her way out. He read all the shiny details of what interested her so much and blinked his dark eyes. Ripping up the flyer into tiny pieces as they fell to the floor, he kept a vacant expression on his face.

Within a matter of seconds, he turned his face into a scowl, with sharp eyes and gritted teeth. He bawled his hand into a fist and punched the kitchen island counter over and over until his hand was raw and bloody.

*** 

Willow knew right away she wanted to read Gone Girl again. It was her favorite thriller novel. She walked the book club building in circles, just people watching and drinking fruit punch with a pinch of vodka she keeps stashed in her purse.

As she turned the corner, a man with dark thick hair grabbed her attention. His appearance was magnetizing to her. Although he was noticeably attractive, he was also not over the top.

A crisp white Beatles t-shirt clung to his slightly buffed up chest. bringing out the emerald-green color of his eyes and that sharp jaw line with just a little stubble of hair perfectly shaping it.

*Not too macho for a little John Lennon. I wonder who his favorite Beatle is?*

He wore gray sweatpants that showed a little tease of his size, and tennis shoes that creased, hinting that he hits the gym every once in a while.

He stood there gazing in confusion at the people dressed as animals while they put on plays for each other. He laughed a little and put his hand over his mouth to cover his smile. He didn't want to seem like he was making fun of them. She looked at the group of furies, then back at him and smiled to herself.

Willow noticed that thick mane of his immediately, though. It was something she always takes note of about people; how their heads look. She feels like it says a lot about a person. And his head told her he took care of himself, and that meant he has pride in his home too. Something Neil didn't give two shits about.

She wanted to feel his thick, almost black hair. She could tell it would be soft and plentiful in her hand. She pictured grabbing a handful as he kissed her neck with his full lips, she also took note of. Not of everyone, just of him. She knew those feelings were wrong, so she shook her head to snap out of it and walked away from the temptation.

\*\*\*

*I can't believe I had thoughts about another man like that. I haven't ever, not since even just dating Neil. So, what the hell was that even about? Get your shit together, Willow. It's not a sin to notice an attractive guy. Ummm, but when you wanna do more than just look… I feel guilty. Maybe I need more to drink. I'm gonna get more to drink.*

As she unscrewed the lid from her secret liquor bottle, she saw him again. And this time he stood near the book she came here for. *Fuck.* She turned around, fast. Then, poured a shot in her cup and downed it, letting the red juice just slightly drip down the sides of her mouth.

After tucking the vodka bottle back into its place, she wiped her face with the back of her hand and felt lighter with the warmth from the liquor in her belly. Turning back to face him, her mind couldn't be stifled.

*Say hi before he does. You're the alpha.*

*Wait, is he looking at me? Just pretend you don't notice that too much and go fucking say hi.*

# Pauleen

I simply adored my sweet neighbor, Willow. I remember the first time I ever met her. She reminded me so much of my daughter. Tillie passed away when she was only twenty-two years old.

A drunk driver hit her and my life fell into shambles. When Willow and Neil moved into their apartment, I saw it as a sign to finally be close to my daughter again. She even dressed like Tillie did.

She wore floral patterned, flowy dresses with sandals when it was Summer and Spring. In the winter and fall time, she wore leggings with oversized sweaters and boots. Her spiral curly blonde hair and brown eyes match Tillie's picture I keep on the mantle in my living room. Their resemblance to each other was striking.

Having Willow around, just right next door to me gave me the hope I needed to finish out the rest of whatever life that I had left in me. Tillie was my only child, and my husband was in the car with her when that drunk driver hit them. I became a widow and a kid-less mother in one day. Just one day. That's all it took to change my life forever. I've been alone ever since then.

Willow was a sweet girl and my motherly instincts kicked in when I heard her and Neil argue through the walls. These walls are so thin, though. You could almost clearly hear every word said even when they didn't talk too loud or yell at each other.

Sometimes they did yell, and that's when every sound came through extremely clear to me. I turned my television volume down each day to hear them talk. Sometimes it was like a Soap Opera and more entertaining than what was on television at the time.

Every couple has their arguments and disagreements, but I was always on Willow's side when I heard them. I always rooted for her, and I always will. It's not just because she reminds me of Tillie, but it's because there was something very wrong with that Neil guy. Maybe she didn't see it for what it was just yet, but I'd need to take her under my wing to help her out of this situation somehow. I wondered where her mother was.

One day, Neil came to me to buy Xanax and because I have plenty to go around, I sold him quite a bit. I was fine with it all until he asked me to keep it hush hush from Willow.

I'm not too fond of a man lying to his wife or keeping secrets. I told him I'd do it because he seemed so desperate. The poor guy was suffering from tremendous anxiety about work.

*Huh. Yeah right.*

Something told me he was really just a master manipulator. I'd have to find a way to tell Willow about this little drug transaction when I could get her alone, away from that monster she called a *husband*.

Oh boy, if she were my daughter.... I'd let him have it!

I'd chew him out and make him run screaming with his tail tucked between his legs like a puppy. Like the ravage *dog* that he was.

At least she had a husband, though. I'm just a lonely old bat. I look in the mirror, and my reflection shows just that. A lonely old bat not looking for love any further than I could throw it.

I was never one of those women who moisturized my face and with age, I didn't really care at all how the wrinkles took over.

Isn't that part of growing old? Wearing it with pride? *I know I do.*

My wrinkles sit just right. You could probably guess how old I am just by looking at my face. Sixty-two. The lines make patterns like a spider web around my once dark eyes.

The color of them has gotten lighter the older I get. You know how some people have those curvy lines on their forehead when they lift their eyebrows? Yeah, I don't even have to lift mine for them to be as visible as they are. Which is thickly visible.

I don't have many laugh-lines around my mouth, and I suppose that's because I stopped smiling the day my husband and daughter died. My earlobes droop low to my neck, and that part is a little embarrassing to me, but even around the house I just dress them up with the diamond earrings my husband bought me on our seventeenth wedding anniversary.

My hair is a crown of silver. I always thought I'd be one of those old women who would cover it with the dark brown my hair used to be, but I quite like my wisdom showing through like this. I used to be in top notch shape because I'd go jogging every afternoon with my favorite girlfriend, but that all stopped when my family died and I moved to the cheap side of the city.

Now, I stay inside and wear a different colored moo, moo, nightgown every few days with a pair of matching slippers. I have pink, blue, green, white, purple, orange. All in pastels.

Death changes people. There is no getting around that. I just pop another pill, *or two or three or four.* Sometimes I lose track of how many I take in a day, but the high sure does make life a fun little ride for me.

# Neil

Willow scolded me about my hand. I tried telling her it was an accident, but when I was put on the spot about something so *trivial*, I wasn't very good at lying. She saw right through me.

And of course, *Pauleen* came by to see what the racket was. I hid my hand as she asked her nosey ass question. Those walls were too thin. And she needed to get a life.

I had already completed hours upon hours of anger management classes, and my fucking wife wanted me to do more? Granted, Willow didn't exactly *know* that I finished it before.

That was in a different city. A different state. A different life. If she knew about Patricia, I don't think she would have been with me anymore. She definitely wouldn't have married me in the first place. And if she found out, I just knew she'd be asking for a divorce. She'd serve those papers to me faster than Claudia did when she found out about Patricia.

*God.*

Both of those women were nightmares. And now my darling wife was starting to act just like them. It always started out like this.

*"You have anger issues. You need anger management."*

And now all *three* of these bitches had said that to me. But with Patricia and Claudia I didn't try. Not really. I mean, I did the classes because they asked me to but that's about as far as I let them take me down. With Willow, I'd go to the classes *and* whatever else she asked of me. I wouldn't dream of letting her go without a fight. A fight I fought harder than for my ex's.

Patricia and Claudia victimized me. It's amazing how I managed to find two different women and marry them both at different times, when they're exactly the same.

Willow wasn't like them, though. Just because she asked me to do what *they* asked of me didn't mean she was the same. It also didn't mean that I had anger problems. It just meant she wanted to actually fight for our marriage. I'd take the blame for our ruining.

I'd bite the bullet and go back to those stupid fucking classes, because she was worth it. She was worth every hour I'd have to sit eye to eye with people bearing *real* problems.

***

The heat from the sun beamed off the dashboard of Neil's car and scorched his face. When he grabbed for the binoculars, it spit fire to his hand. He turned the car on and let the air conditioner cool off his spyware, holding the neck string out with his pointer finger and thumb away from his body, and his face scrunched up in pain. When he looked up, he saw his wife.

There Willow stood, hand in hand with a beefy brunette. Neil quickly placed the binoculars to his face. He wanted a closer look at this fellow, but it burned his skin a little.

"Fuck!" he screamed and dropped them to the floor.

When he moved his foot, he accidentally kicked them underneath his seat. He searched for them with his hands, bending to fit them under his seat. When he finally found them and placed them to his eyes again, the beefy brunette was out of sight and Willow was walking in the direction of her car, smiling to herself the way she used to about him.

That's when he changed his mind about her being different from his other wives.

***

It was either she really was just like Patricia and Claudia, *or* she was different and I just had to win her back. So, what was it that this jock strap had that I didn't? What was *he* doing that's better than what I did for her? *To* her? God. No.

Don't think about that. I can't. I *won't* let my mind go there. Maybe it was the money. This place looked like it costs a fortune a month.

Waterfalls surrounded by stone and giant leafy fruit trees greet you at the entrance. Yes, fruit trees. Not regular trees. Not bushes. They don't fuck around over here.

They're fucking *fruit* trees. *Who the fuck has fruit trees anywhere close to Chicago? Rich people that don't know what else to spend their money on. That's who.*

A gold painted metal gate blocked my entry into the building, but I followed behind some rich asshole who waved at me, then let me in afterwards when he typed in his fancy little code. There was not a spot on the pavement that needed any work done.

Every tenant had their own garage. Only visitors park under the pavilion. *Peasants.* Flowers were freshly planted at each town home apartment, welcoming Summer and all the rich bastards who lived there. And the buildings were all painted like pastel skittles, skipping colors for each home. Not a paint chip could be seen.

*Jesus, Willow. What the hell kind of a man do you really want? What the fuck does this guy do for a living?*

# Brock

I knew Willow would come back to me. She always did. She had tried this before, a few times now. But this time it felt so real. This time she actually went several days without talking to me. This time she actually cried and told me not to call her again when I called her after those few days were up.

This time she opened a message I sent her on Instagram and left me on read. She had never done those things the other times she said we had to *keep it at the book club*. I thought I had lost her for good. I wasn't ready to give her up. Neither one of us could stay away from each other for very long. We couldn't even explain it. It was just the chemistry we had. We were bound to each other forever.

And, we both knew this.

\*\*\*

"I can't not come over when you invite me to." Willow whispered into his ear.

He could feel the warmth of her breath and smell a faint sense of vodka and coconut lingering from her mouth. As he caressed her naked back, she lay on her stomach facing him, wearing a cheesy grin and biting her bottom lip.

She blushed a little and covered her face with the blanket. He pulled it off her face and ran the back of his hand over her cheek.

"And I can't not invite you over." Brock admitted, smiling back at her.

When they made love their bodies fit together like puzzle pieces. Like they were created specifically for each other. It was as if they were destined to be one at last. He didn't care that she was married.

He'd take whatever he could get from her; whatever she could give him. He knew Willow's marriage was falling apart. She told him as much. He also knew she felt stuck, trapped with her husband and he knew this could happen to women. So, he was okay with being her *side guy* for now.

It wouldn't be much longer that he would need more out of her.

# Willow

Brock was my person. He saved me from the unnecessary drama and arguments with Neil. He made me laugh harder than I ever had with anyone else, *including my husband.*

Neil used to really get me going. It was him who, in the past was the one who had made me laugh harder than anyone else. At this time in our marriage, even when he tried his best at getting me to laugh or smile, I just didn't find him funny anymore. It's like when you're in love with someone and all of their flaws aren't even relevant to you at the time.

Love is blinding. Well, it's the opposite when you fall out of love with someone because of how much you grow to dislike them. Everything you used to love or like about that person starts to become almost like a flaw and unattractive. You just feel nothing.

I was having a full-blown affair with Brock, then. I didn't really know how to take that. *I am a cheater.* It all happened so fast to be honest. I had broken my vows. Every single one of them. But at the time, I couldn't have said I was regretful. Neil wasn't who I thought he was.

He became an angry, chauvinist pig of a man. He was secretive with just about everything then, *and perhaps always had been.* I was a stranger to him; as he was to me. He wasn't always like that, though. His gentle side vanished the moment we got back from our two-week long honeymoon in the Caribbean.

\*\*\*

"And, just where the fuck do you think you're going this late at night, Willow?" Neil demanded to know, following her through their bedroom as she went back and forth from the closet to her vanity to get all primped up for her evening out with Brock.

"Oh, so you can have your secrets, but I can't?" She rolled her eyes and buckled the strap of her high heels around her ankles.

"So, it's a secret? It's a secret where you're going, eh?" He smiled, but not the happy kind of smile. It was a *you're such a little bitch* type of smile. You know that kind of smile. Everyone does.

"I didn't say that. And, don't talk to me this way. *I'm your wife!*" She yelled this at him, with red lipstick covering only her bottom lip, and the lipstick wand still in her hand up to her mouth as she peered at him through the mirror of her vanity.

At this Neil laughed hysterically, bending over with his hands placed on his thighs, as if to hold himself up from a belly laugh that he just can't seem to stop. He put his hand up and between laughter he said, "Oh…. my... God. Willow. Don't make me laugh."

Willow smacked her lips together to cover both her top and bottom lips with that bright red, pinup style lipstick. She shook her head and threw her purse over her shoulder, and grabbed her car keys from the hook beside the front door. With tear filled eyes she told him goodbye for the evening.

*** 

Neil's behavior was just so odd to me. He would laugh at things that aren't funny. Like when we went to my aunt's funeral, he couldn't control himself from laughing almost the entire trip there and back. He played it cool around my family. But then during the drive, I sat in the passenger seat wondering what kind of a man I married.

"What the fuck is so funny, Neil?"

"Huh? Oh. Um. Nothing."

And, his Joker sounding laughter carried on.

I had never seen anyone act so weird before. I wasn't sure if this was just how he mourned a death or if he was one of those people who laughed during nervous type of situations.

But it was something about his laughter. Something that told me this asshole genuinely thought my aunt's death was funny, or that people hurting so much inside was hilarious to him. I just wasn't too sure of what it was that made him cackle like that, but it was one of the creepiest things I had ever witnessed. How do you confront something like that? What else do you do other than ask why and tell him to stop?

I just did what started to become *me* around him. I said nothing, *again*. And again, nothing is what I would say to him a lot. Nothing is what eventually took over me around him.

Because I was scared of him; of what he might do, I transformed into a silent wife. Brock turned my volume up. He brought me back to life. I needed him.

# Pauleen

"I didn't say that. And don't talk to me this way. *I'm your wife!*" Loud and clear as day I heard Willow yell this through these paper-thin walls in this ghetto, dirt cheap apartment building. I popped another Xanax and waited for it to kick in before I would knock on their door.

When I heard Neil laughing. No, when I heard him *cackling like a Devil,* I popped another Xanax and zipped up my night gown all the way. I didn't want anyone to see any part of my chest. I put my slippers on, that sat at the foot of my fluffy recliner. Neil's cackling grew louder and I thought I heard a door slam.

I was about to make my way over to check on them and instead I peeked out the curtains of my kitchen window that showed a view of the parking lot. Willow was wiping tears off her cheeks. She looked stunning, though.

She wore a pink, knee length dress covered in multi-colored flowers. Her hair was even more curly and bouncier than usual, like she had just got it done at the salon. Instead of her normal sandals or flats, she wore heels that sparkled under the streetlights. I wondered where she was going. It always made me nervous when she'd walk to her car at dark time around these parts.

*It's Chicago, for crying out loud!*

I watched over her until she got in her car and started it. When she pulled out of the parking lot, I felt a little bit better about her safety. Neil was no gentleman. He should have walked her to her car, even if he was mad at her. Anger doesn't halt the *action* of real love. Possession is what he had for Willow.

# Neil

Neil began to make it a habit to follow Willow on the nights she went out past the curfew he tried to give her.

"You're insane if you think I'm following *a curfew*." Willow laughed at him.

"Don't think of it as a demand. You'll drive yourself mad thinking that way. Instead, think of it more like a way of showing appreciation towards all I do for you." Neil held out a hand like he was offering her something.

She rebelled against his wishes and ran straight into Brock's arms each time she left home after her work hours.

\*\*\*

Patricia and Claudia were not *this* difficult. Sure, they gave me one hell of a hard time trying to leave me. Both of them did. They each lacked any remorse for their actions. And if I didn't know any better, I'd call them both sociopaths.

*Is Willow a sociopath, too?*

No. Get that out of your head. Willow isn't a sociopath. She's just more hardheaded and stubborn; an alpha. It's actually one of the things I fell in love with about her.

She had taken it too far now this time, though. She needed to be put back in her place and know her role. She was mine. And I was hers. When we made a vow, we *bought* each other. The price comes with a lifetime of humiliation. I had to show her who the fuck was boss.

\*\*\*

I had the beefy brunette's address memorized now. Brock was his name, so I had learned by searching his address online. You can get anyone's information for just a buck online nowadays. Or even for free.

Ya know.

Just follow your whore wife on her little cheating spree and it won't take long if she's as stupid as mine was. You'll get his address, then just Google search it. The asshole's name will pull right up.

Wanna get further?

Hell, just pay the dollar a month and you can get unlimited access to all his shit.

Willow would take a little trip there after she got off work sometimes. I hadn't confronted her about this just yet. I'd rather her to come clean to me about her cheating and lies.

I wanted her to snap the fuck out of it and realize what she had done to us. I dreamed of her crawling to me as I back away. *A little game I'll play.* And I wanted her to beg for my forgiveness. Of course, I'd forgive her.

But I wanted to see her at my mercy first. I wanted to see her face turn and her pretty brown eyes evolve to blood shot red because she's crying so much and pouring the guilt out of her like the callous woman she had become.

She didn't do any of that. Instead, she continued on doing whatever it is they did behind Brock's perfectly polished closed door. I couldn't bring my mind to think of what they did.

*No, I won't go there.*

I had to stop her from digging this hole deeper than it already was.

# Willow

Brock understood me. He didn't pressure me to have kids. Not that he could really. I mean, I was a married woman after all. But he even said he would never in the future. I liked that.

He saw a future with me, and it didn't involve children who would indefinitely suck the life out of both of us. Neil didn't get it. His parents were picture perfect; present for every occasion, with wide smiles and long, lasting hugs.

Neil and his siblings were everything to them. *They live for their children.* But my parents are not like that. I watched my mom and dad as I grew up. And I saw my mom's dreams and aspirations of being a lawyer fade into the abyss. They disappeared along with her. She settled as a stay-at-home mom turned to housewife. She was always absent minded and inpatient with me; with my dad too.

My mom was always late to my spelling bees. *When she even showed up.* She knew those were so important to me. I wasn't the girl who danced in ballet or cheered for the football team. I was the kid who liked reading, and spelling bees were my thing every year.

I was also in UIL (University Interscholastic League), and she was absent for all of those events too. It baffled me that she wanted a grandchild, but maybe she wanted a do over. She could show love to a newborn she'd borrow a few times a month. That would be easy for her.

It wasn't so easy when she had to force herself to smile at me when I shared something I thought was cool, growing up. And while my dad was there, he wasn't really. He was distant; standoffish.

*Good job* is all he would say when I'd tell him an achievement of mine, then clear his throat like a tick he has when he's nervous or anxious to move onto the next thing.

It's inevitable we all end up like our parents. We can become them if we're not careful. So, why would I want kids? To pass this unbreakable cycle off to them? No, thank you.

***

"My childhood was shit, too." Brock related.

"Spill the juicy stuff," she loved hearing his husky foreign accent and watching his hand movements he'd make to abstract the story even more.

"Well, my job doesn't exactly pay much, to be honest. It's more like spending money, to me. My parents have me set for life."

He looked at Willow's face to gauge her reaction and he noticed she didn't move closer to him or arch her back to show off what she's got up there. A lot of women did things like that when he'd tell them he had money.

"Uh.... with money that is. But that's all they can offer, is money. No affection. No, *I love you's*. They just pay my way. My father is a doctor. My mother is a psychologist. They're too busy for me and my sisters, but they *do* have money. And that's the way they show their love, I guess."

Willow raised her eyebrow and smirked at him.

"Look. I know it sounds like the life to a lot of people, but it's actually lonely as fuck. I wouldn't want to bring a child into my world. Their grandparents wouldn't even care to know her or him anyway. They don't even know what my job is or where I live. They just sign that check over." He made a hand motion like he was holding a pen and writing.

"Did you have a nanny growing up? Were you one of *those* kids?" She sat Indian style on his couch, Willow listened intently. She laughed when she said this.

Brock groaned, then let out a little laugh "I suppose I was one of *those* kids."

"Soooo, carry on. What were you like as a kid? What were you into? What did you plan to be when you grew up? Tell me everything. Tell me it all." Willow took a bite out of an apple and covered her mouth as it crunched.

"Honestly? I know it might sound stupid, but I wanted to be just like my dad."

"That doesn't sound stupid at all." Willow playfully pushed Brock's arm. "Why would you even say that?"

"My dad just didn't have time for me. He was too involved in his work. Still is. Because I wanted to be just like him *or perhaps gain his approval, should I say…* I'd listen along with whoever he'd be talking to on the phone about medicine and such. When I got older, I started to actually study medicine, and everything else he did. I even learned a little bit of how to perform childbirth. *Weird, I know.* He kind of dabbled in it all, so I kind of studied it all."

"How come you didn't finish college?"

"He didn't give a shit, so I just stopped. I started doing what I like to do instead. I like to build things."

"Ah. I see."

She was then laying against the back on the couch they sat on and had her legs propped over his lap. She wore a sheer floral dress, like she had many times around Brock. Her sandals were off and he studied her pink painted toenails, then ran his hand up her leg.

"And what about you?" It was Brock's turn to be nosey then.

"What do you mean what about me?"

"Tell me something nobody knows." Brock teasingly tickled her leg, then smiled. She laughed and squirmed around. "Tell me something not even your husband knows."

Willow smiled back at him, closed mouth and played with her hair. She looked up to the ceiling. "Hmmmmm"

"Oh, come on. Don't be shy. *Spill the juicy stuff.*" Brock said in a girly voice to mimic Willow.

"Okay. I have high blood pressure and—"

Willow took another bite out of her apple and opened her mouth like she was about to talk more. She then closed it and covered her mouth again with her hand and giggled a little. She held her pointer finger up to indicate 'one minute'.

"Why would your husband not know you have high blood pressure? Seems like a silly thing to keep from him and other people." Brock chuckled.

Then, he saw she had her finger up and he placed both his hands in the air like he was showing free hands to a police officer. "Okay, okay. You got more. Spill it. After you finish chewing, of course"

47

Willow swallowed her bite. "Sorry," she laughed again. "Okay. So, I have high blood pressure and that causes issues with taking birth control. So, I'm not on birth control."

"Oooh. That makes a bit more sense now. Still, why doesn't your husband know about this, or your parents or your friends?"

"Because I just don't tell my friends a lot of really anything." She looked down, embarrassed that her friends weren't the type you could count on. "My mom would have a complete heart attack if she knew I even *thought* about birth control, and Neil... my husband."

She sat up from her legs laying on his lap, and shifted in her seat. She shook her head. "I didn't tell him before we got married because he always seemed to be in the mindset as me about living free, with no kids. I didn't need to tell him. Ya know? It was no big deal. We just wrapped it up every time. But after we got married and he started begging me for babies, I for sure kept that a secret. I just don't trust him. How could I?"

Brock gazed at her with a drunk in love look. Willow didn't think he really heard her. She felt like he might have been just admiring her beauty and blocking out all she said. Many men had done this in her company.

"That's okay. I don't expect you to understand." Willow shrugged.

"Oh, I do. I understand completely." Brock moved closer to her on the couch and wrapped his arms around her, then kissed her on the forehead.

# Brock

Willow was profoundly beautiful. She was the most real person I knew. We would talk about everything. From jokes that made our sides ache from the laughter, to our deepest and darkest nightmares and secrets.

I took pictures of her using my Nikon camera as she twirled around in her flowy dresses. My camera was professional gear, but the subject is what makes the picture count for a thousand words. She took selfies with me using her cellphone. We made funny faces and fed each other snacks in the ones she took.

All of our memories were compiled together in zipped lock files placed on my computer to print. I had planned to matte them in frames and hang them in spots she'd pick out in my apartment. Her double life with me had become my one, main sole purpose. I lived, ate and breathed Willow. She was my addiction.

I wanted to tell her I love her, but the thought of her not saying it back had me holding off for just a bit longer. I knew she felt it. Her eyes told me she did. But would she actually say it?

We had been seeing each other for nearly seven months then, and I just couldn't get enough of her. I'd keep her here forever with me if she'd let me. But the night ends with us and she always had to go home to her husband. I felt like shouting out profanities when she got dressed to leave. I told her this, and she stopped mid movement of clamping her bra.

"Hey. We might need to spend some time apart." she starred off in the distance, like she was taking in what I had just said to her.

Hopping up out of bed, barefoot and only in my boxers, I jogged towards her, "Whoa, whoa, whoa. Hold up a minute. Why though?"

"Maybe we're spending too much time together, ya know?" She put her shirt on.

"No," I laughed. "No, we're not. Look. If you're worried about me catching strong feelings or something, you can be at ease to know

49

that my guard is up also. Just like you, Willow." pleading as my face followed hers at every turn she moved to look away from me.

I finally gently placed my hand under her chin and moved her face to see my eyes. "It's okay, Willow. We don't have to take a long break. You know? I'll give you your space. I'll be here when you're ready."

She looked into my eyes and tears made a little home in hers. "Okay" and she shook her head in agreement, wiped her tears away, then pressed her hand against my heart on my chest. "I'll see you soon."

# Neil

My wife had taken off *again*. At least this time she wasn't with Brock (Aka Fuck Boy). I knew this because she told me she needed space. Oh, I didn't just trust her words. Hell no.

I kept my car at a distance and saw her park at *and* go into a coffee shop alone. She nearly noticed I was watching her. I had to duck down in my seat real fast when she stopped walking in the middle of the street and turned around, looking towards my direction. It was a close call, but my Willow didn't catch on.

When I reversed out of the parking lot, I saw him. There was *Brock*, in his shiny new looking corvette. He was just sitting in there doing nothing other than staring at the coffee shop my wife had just walked into.

Fumes of anger filled inside me as I grabbed my phone to call her and ask for an explanation.

*Is she really fucking meeting him here? She'd be one ballsy bitch. Everyone who works here knows she's married. They've seen us here together a hundred times.* I pulled back into the parking spot and sat and watched him watch her for a bit before dialing her number. She had grabbed a latte and a muffin, and was hanging outside at a picnic table alone, scrolling through her phone.

*He's not meeting her here. He's stalking her! What a douche bag. He won't do shit, though. He's clearly a pussy. Little fuck boy just sits in his car, hoping the woman of his dreams will talk to him. Fucking loser.*

And on the note that my wife was being good for once, I reversed out of the drive again.

I am a good husband, so I gave her the alone time she asked for and drove back home to get busy cooking her favorite dish; *pasta chicken alfredo!* She normally did all the cooking around here. But it was my turn to spoil her with a four-course meal. She had earned it. I'd pick up a bottle of wine and have all the goodies laid out for her to be

51

surprised when she got home. Maybe Red Box had a good movie to rent. We'd have a romantic night in. I'd remind her why she married me *and* why she needed to stay.

***

I cooked all this fucking food, rented Gone Girl (*her* favorite movie), bought flowers, chocolate, and a charm to add to her collection for that stupid necklace she wore every day. Willow never came back home.

*Fucking Brock.*

I guaranteed that's where she was at; little fuck boy's house. Having his address benefited me that night more than ever. I grabbed my keys from the hook and dropped them.

*Shit.* No time to lose. Confrontation hour was upon us.

# Willow

Pacing the back field of Brock's apartment complex was a little intrusive of me, but I needed to find myself. In the city there isn't much country life. There is nowhere to go to collect your thoughts. It's all street signs bossing you around, the latest shopping trends daring you to spend your last dollar on, as it wears perfectly on a mannequin, then flimsy on your body.

People shove past each other on sidewalks and don't even bother to say excuse me. It's easy to get mugged in broad daylight with people carrying on about their business, even though they just witnessed the act. Everyone is busy in the city of Chicago. Don't get me wrong, I love the packed community of the drifters playing music for a buck outside of restaurants, the entrepreneurs passing out their business cards to any and every one *"Buy my stuff"*, the important people who moved up in the world wearing all black and chatting deadlines on their cells, using the street as an office as they blindly stroll pass me, and not giving a damn who hears what they say.

Just outside my apartment building, all of this scenery resurrected each day. I enjoy a little grit in my life. I really did. But I needed a breather from it all right then. And even though Neil and Brock were suffocating me with pressure, I somehow found myself here.... in Brock's backyard. My heart had led me to him even in my attempt at breaking away just for a day.

\*\*\*

Two deer trot along right before Willow's eyes and she couldn't believe it. The mother and her fawn. She quickly took her cellphone out of her purse and snapped multiple pictures of them. Uploading them to Instagram, she didn't tag her location like she normally did.

She captioned it *Doe a Deer, a Female Deer! Name that song!* And ended that with a green heart emoji she signatures every post with.

Putting her phone back into her bag, she watched them prance off together and blend in with the trees that lay ahead of her. Moving branches out of her way, she followed them into the wooded area.

# Brock

Willow didn't know that I had followed her everywhere she tried going to for peace and quiet that day. I just wanted to make sure she was okay, that's all. Alright, and I missed her. She told me she needed space, but she ended up right back at my house. She didn't need time to herself.

She needed *me*.

It was evident. There she was, strolling around in the field behind my town home complex, like it was hers too. I'd let her move in with me if that's what she wanted. She could pick which side of the bed is hers, take any dresser drawers she pleased, stock the pantry with whatever food she craved. She could have it all. I would give her the world.

Anything she desires would be hers.

She knew I would see her in the field. So, I wondered if this was a test? If I didn't go to her, she'd hold it against me and I'd never be forgiven for abandoning her in such a time of need.

If I did go, and she didn't want me to, then I'll have crossed her boundaries. What to do? Man, women can be complicated to read sometimes. But I obeyed my gut feeling and started in her direction. I'd rather her tell me to fuck off for a little while than to not trust I'll be there for her any time she's going through some thing hard.

This time when I followed her, I let her see me do it.

# Neil

Speeding through red lights faster than a bat out of hell, Neil almost hit a couple crossing the street and swerved to miss them. He nearly caused a wreck when he swerved to miss the couple. His eyes widened and his heart pounded.

He pulled into a parking spot in front of a pub and rested his head against the seat. He panted and peeved until the heavy breathing subsided, then he started laughing. He howled out with adrenaline and slapped the steering wheel.

"Whew!" he yelled out.

He shook his head violently to release some of the left over high from the near death he almost caused for multiple people. He hit the steering wheel again, and slapped it over and over while howling an angry laughter, if there ever was one. Grabbing the keys from the ignition, he had worked up an appetite for beer. He stumbled into the pub, still high with adrenaline and took a seat at the bar.

"What can I get ya?" A young man covered in colorful tattoos made a race with pouring whisky in shot glasses standing in rows, on the other side of the bar. One of the tattoos showing on his hand was of a woman's name, *Liz* in all caps and there was a line marked through it.

*Guess he regretted that date.*

"I'll take a tall boy." Neil got out his wallet.

"Of what?" the bartender asked with a chipper voice. *Big drinks equal big tips.*

"Oh. Ummm. Miller Light." He read the drinks on tap.

"Coming right up!" the bartender chirped again.

"Open a tab for me, will ya?" Neil laid his credit card down on the bar.

"Sure thing!" that chipper voice came back once more.

By the end of his binge drinking, he tipped the bartender hefty and headed home, feeling like the good guy that he just knew he was.

# Willow

Neil didn't know it, but his mom told me he was married before. I hadn't been the same towards him since then. I was stiff around him. Quiet. A silent wife.

How could he have kept such a big secret from me? I had thought about bringing it up several times before. But a man who could keep something that big from someone he *says* he loves couldn't be trusted with anything. He'd come up with some stupid excuse for not telling me and *I'll* be labeled the bad guy for not forgiving him.

Because how else could I learn anything different than what he would say?

His mom didn't provide any more information and she asked me to not tell the rest of their family that I knew this. I kept my mouth shut, not wanting to cause any problems for her.

Asking my own mom for advice didn't help me at all.

"Momma. What would you do if you found out daddy was keeping a secret from you?" I stood at the entrance of her bedroom door that I'm not allowed to enter when she's laying down in bed.

I visited them for a few days when Neil went out of state to an event for work. Chicago was home, but not when I was alone. I didn't like being alone. At that point, I couldn't go to Brock's town home to stay overnight; let alone a few nights. We hadn't started our affair just yet. We were only friends at the time.

"Everyone has secrets, Willow." She kept her eyes shut, with a wet washcloth rested upon her forehead.

"Okay and I get that. But what if this secret was a deal breaker?" I rolled my necklace charm against my chin.

Sighing, she came back with, "Willow, give Neil a break, would ya? Nobody's perfect." She fluffed her pillow, then tossed it back in its place. She shifted positions in the bed and pulled the wet washcloth down to cover her eyes. "Good God, child. Can't you ever just be *happy* with what you get?"

"I—"

"Can you just close the door and leave me alone? You've given me even more of a headache."

I never brought it back up to her again.

# Brock

Willow's husband was a punk ass bitch. He saw me *watching* her at the coffee shop and he didn't even say shit to me. I knew it was him because I had seen pictures of them together on her phone.

What kind of a husband doesn't kick the guy's ass his wife is having an affair with while they're sitting in the same parking lot? He looked right at me! I knew he knew, exactly who I was. He was the definition of a pussy. Willow deserved so much better than that piece of shit she called a husband. I could give that to her.

She had to leave him, though. Like she kept saying she would. She would have to give *all* of herself to me. She would have to commit to me, and me only.

\*\*\*

Walking through the field behind Brock's apartment complex, he caught a glimpse at Willow jogging to catch up with a pack of deer. She held her phone out and made cooing sounds she thought would beckon them over to her. He figured she'd hear him scuffling behind, but she carried on in oblivion.

Brock kind of enjoyed that she didn't notice him lingering behind her. He could watch her in her element of innocence, see the way she smiles when she didn't think anyone was watching, and just take in all of Willow that he admired.

He followed Willow's trail and began jogging faster than her to witness her giddiness, while peaking at her between the branches of the trees that blocked his view.

When he finally got to her, she lifted her bag into the air and whacked him over the head. He leaned down to cover his head with his hands to shield her from hitting him again.

"Willow, it's me! It's Brock!"

"Oh my God! I'm so sorry! I thought you were just some weirdo guy following me," bending to his level, she grabbed his shirt to pull him towards her. She ran her hand over his head and started laughing, then covered her mouth and bellowed out a giggle again. At that, he matched her laughter and grabbed her hand that covered her mouth.

"Don't hide that pretty smile." he uttered in that foreign accent she couldn't resist, kissing her hand. He watched her face flush red and smiled a little at her.

"Jesus, Brock. You scared me. What are you *doing* out here?"

"What are *you* doing out here?" he laughed.

She pulled her hand back from his, and looking down she bit her nail. "I don't really know to be honest."

"Well, you must be starving. It's dinner time. Come on. I'll order us Chinese."

He held his hand out and waited for her to give in. And she did. The sound of his voice was low; patient. She grabbed his hand and held onto it as he guided her to his town home apartment.

***

"I have my alarm set. But don't forget to wake me up just in case." Willow breathed. "We know that if Neil wakes up in the morning and I'm not there, all hell will break loose. I can't handle it."

She lay in bed beside Brock, with a full belly, feeling the breeze from the fan caressing her stripped body. He watched her sleep off the booze for a little while; studying her chest pump slowly up and down and listened to the rhythm of her breath. Willow was dead asleep.

She had drank all day and night. Now the liquor was working its magic and sedating her completely. Brock tested this as he poked her shoulder a few times, whispering her name. Then he shook her lightly and it still didn't wake her. He kissed her lips, and moving to her cheek he continued to her neck. She stayed fast asleep.

He reached over her and grabbed her phone from the nightstand that lay beside her. Turning her cell phone on, he pressed the code seven-four-seven-four and the screen came to life to his eyes.

He mimicked the steps she took to get to her alarm and slid the one she set for just a few hours from then to the off setting. He pushed the side button to return back to the home screen and reached across her again to lay it back down on the nightstand. He needed her to get plenty of uninterrupted sleep for the busy night he had planned for them.

# Neil

Waking up with a hangover is not for the faint-hearted. My head throbbed and beat against every piercing thought that came through. *Willow isn't home.* Her side of the bed was empty.

Walking to the window to open the blinds felt like a workout. Every inch of my body ached and cracked as I hunched over and stepped into the living room area. She wasn't on the couch either.

*Where the fuck is my wife?*

The nice dinner I cooked for her still settled on the dining table, waiting to be feasted. The sight of it made me queasy. And the smell lingered, filling my nose with a stench too strong to stomach. I gagged, then covered my mouth with both hands and ran to the kitchen sink and threw up all the pity I drank of myself from the night before.

***

Looking through the medicine cabinet for Ibuprofen to gnaw off this headache that crept into my temples, footsteps stormed outside my front door. It sounded like someone stomping around in boots.

It was almost as if they were doing this on purpose; just to be annoying. Like they knew I was suffering with the pounding hangover headache of a lifetime. Then, a few knocks at my door beat through my ears and I quickly swallowed the pills. I headed off to see what my nosey ass neighbor wanted this time.

"What can I do ya for?" *Jesus. Why do I talk like that sometimes?*

Pauleen peeked inside behind me "I noticed Willow's car isn't outside. Is she okay?"

Moving to block her view through the space behind, *I'm not hiding anything. It's just none of her fucking business.* "That's very nice of you to check in on us Pauleen, but she's fine and on her way home."

This bitch just blinks at me. Like I *owe* her some type of explanation. "Yeah, I called her." I held up my cell phone "She's literally on her way right now."

She stuttered, "Oh, okay. You guys let me know if ya need anything." she was still trying to peer around me.

"Sure. Thanks." I closed the door in her face as she opened her mouth to say one last thing.

*Bye Karen.*

\*\*\*

The cold water felt like knives stabbing me, but I had to wake up. An ice-cold shower would do the trick. I needed to be alert and ready for whatever bullshit would be thrown my way. Willow crossed the line on way too many levels this time, and that slut had it coming.

# Pauleen

One pill. Two pills. Three pills. Four. Four was my lucky number. Willow hadn't made it home yet, and my nerves were in shock. I needed to drown them out. She had stayed out all night long. I had hoped she was having the time of her life with her friends.

Maybe she was partying up, like I remember doing when I was young and full of spunk. She looked like she was going to a fancy dinner party, but I didn't notice her have any overnight bag with her, other than her purse she carried with her every time she left on an average day.

You know how young people are, though. They'll go drinking all night long, not even prepared to brush their teeth the next morning at the party house or hotel or wherever they end up waking up the next morning.

It was eight forty-five a.m. and I had been waiting for her to get home for three hours then. I woke up at five-thirty every morning, and each day I would open up the curtains to let the sun light shine through the windows.

I didn't have much of a scenery to admire, but I always noticed Willow's car parked out front during these hours. Even on the weekdays. She didn't leave for work until around ten in the morning most days.

On this day, her car was gone.

I couldn't find my slippers anywhere in the living room, and I was in too much a rush to go looking in my closet for another pair. So, I put on a pair of boots I had sitting by my front door.

They were covered in mud and a bit too big for me. They used to be my husband's boots, and I just couldn't part with them. Having them placed by my front door made me feel like he'd come walking through the door any moment now.

Maybe that's not a healthy coping mechanism. I had heard that from my therapist, but it was working just fine for me. I'd never stop coping and mourning the loss of that man.

Neil's car was parked out front, but Willow's wasn't and I needed to know why. Had he done something to her? Had he killed her and disposed of her car *and her body*?

Had he found her in the middle of the night and locked her away in some underground dungeon he built for a time like this? I took another Xanax. These thoughts wouldn't stop spiraling out of control. They popped up in front of me like thought bubbles with the accusations written in all caps.

The pills had finally kicked in, and my anxiety was put a little to rest. I knocked on Willow's door and Neil answered. He told me she was on her way back home and that he had just gotten off the phone with her, but I didn't believe him. I tried peeking around him and the door to see inside their apartment.

I wanted to see if the furniture was still in place or if there was any broken glass on the floor. He had blocked my view, though. I was about to ask him if he'd tell Willow to come knock on my door when she got home, but he slammed the door right in my face.

He had done something to her. I just knew it.

# Willow

"You said you'd wake me up!" Willow screeched at Brock as she paced around his bedroom.

"I'm sorry. I must've slept in along with you," lighting a joint, he watched her as she fumbled around in her jeans only, looking for her bra and shirt.

"This is not okay, Brock! You said—" but he interrupted her.

"Look. It's an accident. Okay?" He sat up on the edge of the bed and peered down at his feet.

"No. Okay. You're right. I'm sorry. It's not your fault. It's not anybody's fault." lightening up, she trudged to him and spread his legs apart with hers, then pressed her breast against his face.

Giving him a little *I'm sorry for being a bitch* hug. He stroked his free hand up her back, then back down to the waist of her jeans. Feeling her soft skin turned him on, and he grabbed her ass, smacked it and stuck out his tongue to taste her tits.

"I gotta go," she interrupted him filling her body up. He let go of her then, but held onto her jeans belt loop and watched her get pulled back as she walked away. She turned to face him and wore an expression of annoyance. He let her go again. But he knew it wouldn't be long before she would be back in his bed.

\*\*\*

On the drive home, Willow listened to Love Fool by The Cardigans and related to her begging for her sweetheart to say those three little words. She was too scared to say it first to Brock.

She was afraid of rejection; of the silence that might follow. The words *I love you, too,* were scarce in her childhood. She'd want to crawl on her mother's lap and listen to her read a book.

As a little girl, she'd daydream of her mother answering all of her silly little questions. She wanted so badly, *and still does* to hear her mother say *I love you* back to her.

But she didn't get what other kids had, and she was taught to appreciate the bare minimum of affection. For this, she would suffer a lifetime of heartbreak; one man after another pretending to love her. She couldn't have faced it if Brock was like that, too.

She'd rather have left things the way they were and just ride it out. The man she married proved to be the same as all the others. Actually, he had proven to be *worse* than all the others.

And because of her mom, because of her friends, because of Neil's off-putting behavior... she was stuck with him. She was trapped in a world nobody could break through, not even her.

She thought about how young she was; only twenty-four years old. She knew she had a long hellacious road ahead of her to be staying put like this. There was just no way she could do it any longer.

At the thought of that, Willow slapped the power knob of the car radio and drove the rest of the way home in silence. Tears poured down her makeup smudged face, leaving black clumps of mascara around her eyes and lines dropping down her cheeks, like vertical cat whiskers.

She turned beat red. Her heart rate increased with rage. She tried to breathe the rage out and rid of it like she wanted to with Neil. But it took over like a growing infection, spreading everywhere and leaked inside her. She fed it medicine by talking it down, *you're better than that, Willow.*

But it rejected and settled in her center, claiming a cozy little home from a landlord that keeps taping up eviction notices on the door. And on the rest of the way back to her apartment, she plotted her final escape.

\*\*\*

Walking into her apartment, the smell of stale food rose to the air and hit Willow's nose. She crinkled it in disgust. Last night's uneaten gourmet' meal rested on the dining table.

A half dead, pink carnation bouquet wilted in a vase between the plates of food. The DVD Gone Girl was propped against the vase, and this minor effort tempted her forgiveness to Neil.

She opened the small, purple gift box he wrote her name on top of, and the charm of a book sparkled a diamond at her. She plopped down in a chair at the dining table and cried once again.

Except this time guilt rushed through her, and she sobbed like a baby, giving herself a headache that always creeps in when she cries. Feeling every bit of sorry for herself, she pried apart the box of chocolates left for her and shoved them into her mouth, one after another.

Indulging in all the sappiness laid out for her, she took her necklace off and added the new charm to it, then put it back on and rolled it against her chin like she did when she was nervous.

She thought about this for a second. And she realized that her wearing that charm meant something. That to Neil this would mean they're rekindled. *All is forgiven.* But to her, she just liked the way it shined against her top.

The chocolate was one thing, but this? She knew she couldn't accept it. She knew that if she did, it meant that she also accepted *him* and she didn't. Not anymore. Flashbacks of all that steered her away from him ran like a movie reel in her mind.

She took her necklace off again and huffed as she put the charm back in the box. It was time to end this once and for all. She pulled her phone out to call Neil and when she looked at the screen, he was already calling. She took a deep breath and prepared for what was about to happen.

# Neil

Unless there was some secret parking area I didn't know about, Willow wasn't at Brock's apartment. She wasn't parked under the pavilion where I normally saw her car, and he only had a one car garage.

So, where could my darling wife be? I tried her favorite coffee shop, the one she was at the day before. But no, that would be too easy for me. Of course, she wasn't there. I drove down the street to the pub where she met her friends once a week.

*Bingo!* I saw Stacy's car.

Continuing on with my drive I noticed Anna and Bridgett had parked right beside each other. Willow's car should have been parked in one of those three rows, but it wasn't.

She was missing her weekly meeting with her posse? Or were they taking shots and gossiping without her on purpose? *Probably.* They were probably gossiping *about* Willow. That's just the way they were.

*Wait a second. What time is it? It's still morning time, right?*

I looked down at my watch, and yes it was still morning. Who the fuck drinks at ten a.m.? No wonder she wasn't there.

Okay. No more driving around in search of my wife. I should know where she's at all times anyway. She usually didn't pick up my phone calls anymore, but I tried her cell phone anyway.

"Hey," came through at the second ring.

*Pinch me. Am I dreaming? The ever so busy Willow actually answered her phone. It's a fucking miracle.*

"Hey, you," I said to her, instead of what was really on my mind.

"I'm home. Where are you?" *And just where the hell have you been, Willow?*

"I'm headed there now." I pulled out of the pub parking lot.

"Okay. Well, I'll see you soon then?" *Is that sadness I heard in her voice?*

"Yeah. You okay?" *Like she'd actually tell me.*

"No. Not really. I need to talk to you about... hello? Neil? Hello?"

I wasn't ready to hear it, so I pressed and held a button in her ear until she hung up the phone. She can think we lost connection for all I cared. I'd do whatever it took to not have to hear her say she wanted a separation.

I wasn't stupid. I knew that's why she *actually* picked up my call. But hey, at least she sounded sad. Maybe I could use that to my advantage. A woman as emotional and dramatic as Willow couldn't stand to see a man cry.

I'd get the tears pouring at the drop of a hat if she were to pull this shit when I got home. And if that wouldn't work, I'd have to think quickly of what to do next. Because I'd be damned if she walked out that door again.

Thinking negative was never really for me, though. So I pushed those thoughts to the back of my mind and pulled more positive ones to the surface. Maybe she was ready to come clean.

Perhaps she had broken it off with Brock and had finally snapped the fuck out of it and realized the catch she had at home. And if that was the case, I didn't want her to even have to utter the words of what she had done. I didn't care if she didn't beg at my mercy this time.

There was always more time for that. I just wanted her back, to stay away from Brock and that fucking book club. Because let's face it. If she hadn't gone there, she would have never met him. And if she never met him, she wouldn't have ever cheated on me.

And her friends, I would have liked for her to stay away from them too. Anna influenced her into temptation. I just knew it, and Willow fell into that trap with Brock.

I could forgive that. I really could. I would have moved past this. As long as she stayed with me, I'd do whatever she wants. *Be* whatever she wants. But if she tried leaving me, she had a rude awakening, like Patricia and Claudia had when they tried. I was not letting her go without one hell of a fight.

***

"I knocked on your door earlier, but nobody answered." *Pauleen has way too much time on her hands.*

Swinging my keys. "Well, I'm home now. Is there something you need?"

"Actually, I saw Willow's car and I just wanted to chat. Ya know, girl talk."

"She might be sleeping." I rolled my eyes as she turned her head to look at Willow's car.

"Alright then. Can you tell her I came by?"

"I'll let her know," smiling at her, hoping these niceties would end any second now, even though it had just started.

She held her brown grocery bag delicately, with leafy green vegetables peeking out the top. She got groceries delivered to the curb once a week.

"Alright then," she said again.

Her little slogan: *Alright then.*

She had a bit of a country accent and wore her old age like a badge of honor. I wondered where she was from because you just don't see such a southern belle like her around here, but I didn't ask because she'd yap her mouth until I'd turn skeletal.

When she walked away, I let out a big sigh in relief. She turned back to face me and her face wore a look of concern. She probably heard me, but I paid no attention to her cat call and went to my darling little wife.

# Brock

Syringes lay in a row on his desk. Small bottles of liquid read Morphine on the front of each bottle. He counted the number of medicine bottles and syringes he had stolen from his dad's briefcase, and smiled at his accomplishment.

Brock hadn't put the morphine to use just yet. He didn't need to. Willow drugged herself enough for what he was about to do. She got black out drunk. She made it a little too easy for him.

But he did put one of the syringes to use; in such a way he could keep her forever. He knew she would need all the sleep she could get on this very busy night of theirs', so he turned her alarm off as she slept beside him.

When Willow shared her darkest secret that she would have an abortion if she got pregnant, he could see in her eyes and body language that she just didn't have it in her to go through with something like that.

He knew she would have second thoughts. He also knew motherhood could glow on her. And during all this love triangle drama, he wanted to have her all to himself. This wasn't a crime of passion.

Not to him anyway. This was a way to show his true love without having to say it. Words mean everything in books, but in life actions are what counts. He did this for her, too.

\*\*\*

Willow slept like a tiny kitten curled up in a ball, praying with her hands together and her hair covered her pretty face. I considerately moved her curly, silky locks off her face, then kissed those appetizing lips. Placing my fingers on them to feel the satin, I glided down to her neck, then to her chest and pressed her perky breast together and gave them a little kiss in the middle.

Wanting to plant my face all the way in between them, I let go and watched them bounce instead. Sex wasn't what this was about. But she arched her back and I thought she was enjoying it while she slept.

*My naughty girl.*

I waited for her to be stifled for my next move. When she finally was, I grabbed a hold of her pink lacy lingerie she wore just for me. I knew she did. As I pulled them off her body, I could smell her. Her scent was my obsession. I inhaled and absorbed every bit of her that lingered in the air.

As she lay there completely naked, I watched her sleep for a bit. My best friend. My lover. My soon to be wife and mother of my child. We didn't use condoms, so it would be easy for her to assume I just didn't pull out quick enough. She'd keep the baby, and I'd be able to keep *her* forever.

# Willow

Just a touch of loopy feeling kicked in as Willow cleaned up the mess from the night before. After she got done scraping food into the trash can and washing dishes, she plopped down on their couch to rest from her hangover and noticed a small tear on the center cushion.

Fidgeting with it, she pulled the string to make it larger. Neil walked in and startled her, even though she knew he was on his way home. The thought of having this talk made her sweat. The anxiety and concern for what might happen made her on high alert.

As she jumped, she yanked at the string and cotton flowed out like a stream of water. She grabbed a piece of the cotton to rip apart. When he turned the corner, she quickly stood up. She feared what lengths he would go to keep her.

Neil blinked at her.

"What?!" she held her hands out, accidentally dropping the ball of cotton to the floor. She bent to pick it up and began tearing it into small pieces. A nervous fidget.

Neil had been holding his breath and didn't even realize. He exhaled loudly and threw his hands up, then shoved them into the pockets of his pants.

"Where ya been?" is all, he could seem to get out.

She adjusted the bottom of her blouse and cleared her throat. *Just like daddy.* "We need to talk."

She tried not to show how nervous she was, but Neil could tell. And he would feed off of it.

"Shit. Willow, I don't want to hear it. Whatever you've done, we can move past it. We can just go on with our lives like nothing happened." He snapped his fingers. "Poof! It could be gone, just like that. You don't even have to say you're sorry. But no more secrets. Okay? I can't handle anymore secrets."

Scowling at him, she told on his mom. "Speaking of secrets, I know what yours are. Were you *ever* gonna tell me you were married before me?"

Neil's pupils dilated, then he sat down on the floor, resting his head against the fireplace. "That was a long time ago."

"Look. I get it. Everybody has a past, but not everybody keeps it from their spouse. Talk or I'm walking out the door."

She pointed her finger towards the front door. Her face looked pale and sickly, like all the life had been sucked out of her. She fidgeted with the cotton in her hands and her entire body shook. This was noticeable to Neil.

He quivered his chin and gazed out the window. Forced tears began to flood down his face. "I don't know that I'm ready to talk about it."

*A little game he plays with her.*

She treaded toward him then and halted right in front of where he sat, looking down at him, with her heart pounding in her ears. She wanted to walk away and leave him in his soiled mess. But she couldn't resist fixing his broken heart. At one time she *did* love him.

She sat down with him, "Neil. It's me. You can tell me what happened. *Please.*"

"Willow! Hey! I know you're in there! Can we talk? Will you come out?!" *Fucking Pauleen.* She made a pattern with her knocks. "Yoo-hoo!"

Willow got up to go where she was needed.

"Pauleen! Hi! Listen, right now isn't a good time," Willow stood with the door covering her body.

"Honey. Are you alright?" Pauleen whispered. She looked unsettled and peaked behind Willow to see what she was hiding.

Willow turned around to see if Neil was coming, and when she faced back to the door, Pauleen had taken a few steps closer to her. Willow jumped and let out a nervous laugh.

"Huh? Yes, I'm fine. Sorry. I'll chat with you later, okay? We can have tea or something."

"I'd love that!" satisfied with her upcoming date with Willow, she told her bye and strolled back to her lonely flat.

"You're too nice." Neil came up behind her.

Willow jumped, then straightened her posture and put her chin up. "Let's get back to your secret." She walked back to the living room area.

Neil followed behind her. "I wasn't trying to be deceitful to you. I promise, Willow. That was never my intention." she waited silently for him to continue. "I was only twenty years old. She was nineteen. We got married *so* young. Ya know?" He sniffled and held tears back for show. Willow gave him an empathetic look then. "We fought all the time. She'd call me names, cheat on me, lie to me. She was a drug addict and I tried to help her."

"What's her name?" Willow requested to know.

Neil looked blankly at her and kept quiet for a few seconds. "Claudia" He finally answered.

"Last name?"

He wiped his nose from his forced grieving and shrugged his shoulders. "I don't know. She changed it after we got divorced. She didn't wanna keep my name or her family name, so she changed it to something different. She might even be remarried now. I couldn't tell you what her last name is even if I *wanted* to."

Willow leaned away from him, "Okay". She drew out the 'a' sound. "But you *can* tell me what her maiden, name was."

"Why? It's not what's important anymore. That was my past. You are my now and future."

Willow veered towards him again. "I've been having an affair." she told him. She immediately looked away from his eyes after she said it. She wasn't prepared to witness what darkness would appear in those hollow holes at this information.

"I already know this, Willow. Can't you see? I can forgive you if this is your only time and you break it off with him." quivering his chin again, he pressed the needle in his pocket against his thigh. Real tears sprang to his eyes this time. "I can't lose you, Willow. I just can't."

She pointed her eyes back to him and when she saw him cry, she just knew it was genuine. Her heart felt like it partly belonged to him, but the other half of her told her to run as fast as she could away from him. She wiped his tears away. Victory was his. That's what she wanted him to think anyway.

***

There are many ways to kill someone and never get caught. I knew all about his little drug deal with Pauleen. She just didn't feel comfortable keeping a secret from me.

At least *someone* felt that way. I knew exactly where he kept the stash, too. I could run him a bubble bath and bring him a glass of wine filled with the pills he bought off her.

I could sit on the edge of the tub and watch his eyes roll back as the pills he bought to sedate me take over his body like a possession. He would drown and it'll look like a suicide.

Another way is to catch the apartment on fire and escape while he lies on the bed, again overdosed by those pills I could serve him in sparkling water. My escape would make headline news.

I can see it now. *Woman Escapes House Fire and Becomes A Widow.* I'd receive donations and gifts by the dozens from strangers all over Chicago. *Not everyone is an asshole here.* Insurance would cover the apartment and I could be in a new flat in no time.

The ideas spiraled in my mind like voices berating me. *Do it. Do it now. Kill him. End this.* They taunted me and took over all other noises around. They demanded the forefront over any other thought that would go through my head. Everywhere I turned and everything I did, they followed me around like a shadow.

I wasn't really hearing voices, though. And I wasn't really going to kill my husband.

A woman can fantasize, right?

\*\*\*

"I'll have two double cheeseburgers with all the vegetables except onions. No onions! Oh! And extra mustard, please." Willow licked her lips, gawking at advertisements of cheesy meals in the drive through at Sonic.

"I've *never* seen you eat that much before." Neil laughed.

"First time for everything, right? But like, I've been eating a *lot* here lately. I don't know what's going on with me. Maybe I'm just about to start my period. You know how I crave hard every month." She waved her hand to slap the thought of pregnancy away, even though she was a month late.

\*\*\*

There was no possibility I'd be pregnant by Neil. We hadn't been intimate, in over half a year. Brock didn't even want kids, so he was

82

extremely careful at making sure he did *not* get even close to knocking me up. But accidents can happen. I knew this. I was an accident, too.

# Neil

My Willow was almost all the way back. She understood why I had to put a GPS tracker on her car *and* cellphone. She was earning my trust back one day at a time. I was so proud of how far she had come.

I was starting to feel a little more comfortable with letting her go places alone then, and sometimes I'd even forget to time her. That's how good it started to get with us. I knew it had only barely been two months, but when you know you know. She had started to laugh at my jokes again.

Okay, it wasn't that belly laugh like it was when we first got together, but it was also not silent like it became. We were finally getting somewhere. I didn't have to crush up anymore pills to knock her out just to go through her phone. I admit I did that a few times here and there.

There were no more locks on her phone screen. And she started to leave her phone laying around sometimes. I believed she did that to show her commitment to me. She didn't face away from me at bedtime anymore either. She even kissed me on the cheek the other night.

I tried to move that kiss onto her lips, but she said she wasn't quite ready yet. I could be patient. I could be understanding. These things take time.

*** 

"What?! You keep calling me!" Neil yelled into his cell phone.

"You've been ignoring my calls, sending me to voicemail all the time." his mother wrapped the cord around her fingers. "That's why I called from the house phone."

"Can you think of any reason why that would be, mother?" He paced around the apartment, grabbed a stack of gum out of the junk drawer in the kitchen and tossed a piece in his mouth.

"No sweetheart. Not at all." nerves shot through her.

"Oh *really?* So, my own mother is just… cool with lying to me? Huh. Nice. Real fucking nice." he popped a bubble.

"Neil! Don't you dare curse at me! I'm your mother!" her voice shook.

"You lost your *mother* title when you stabbed me in the back and almost caused me to get a divorce *again*. Just like you did with Claudia. Why mother? Why would you do this *again?* Don't call me anymore! You're dead to me!" He pointed his finger at the phone as he held it up to his face. He gripped his phone and smashed it on the kitchen counter.

***

Neil's first wife, Patricia was a dancer. He met her at the club she stripped at several nights a week. She was young, and so was he. They were just nineteen and twenty years old.

He had gone there with some of his friends one night, even though he'd say the scene wasn't really for him. He claimed he liked a woman with class, but Patricia stood out to him.

She seemed out of place and he could tell she was a newbie there. He was drawn to her because of this. She was broken and he could pick up the pieces that fell a part in her life and help her put them back together. She would be happy to have someone like Neil save her from having to dance for filthy old men every night.

He paid for a VIP room with her and instead of having her dance or do any sexual favors, he paid her to just talk with him. They spent all night getting to know each other.

Patricia didn't want to be a stripper. She just needed the extra cash to get out of the hell house she was living in with people who used to be her friends. Neil was in awe of her. He found her beauty to be mesmerizing.

She had long blonde hair, that he later found out was a wig and her real hair was short like a bob cut and pitch black. She had Betty Page bangs, and everyone told her she could pull that look off.

He liked the way she looked even more after she pulled off the wig and shook her real hair around. She had ice blue eyes and always drew on cat eyes eye liner that made them look bigger, even when she wasn't dancing at the club. Her skin was a porcelain white color and she was tall and thin.

Neil met up with Patricia a few times at the club after that night and she began to see him as her knight in shining armor. She'd feel relieved when he'd walk through those doors because she knew she could keep her clothes on, and he paid her just for conversation.

It was nice; a breath of fresh air to her. Pretty soon, he got down on one knee in the VIP room and proposed to her. She didn't even care that it was a strip club he popped the question in. She still saw it as romantic because he was saving her from this life. She moved in with him the next day and as long as she was with him, she'd never have to take her clothes off for money again.

Neil bought her a few outfits that were acceptable to him for her wear out in public, and helped her get a job in the cafe at the junior college he was attending at the time. They were a happy married couple.

She met his family and they immediately accepted her with open arms. She didn't have family around for him to meet. They were either dead, lived out of state or had written her off or she had written them off. She really did come from a broken family.

He didn't take much time before he showed his true colors to her after they got married. She was different than Willow in the sense that she wouldn't ever become a silent wife.

She was wild and would fight if she needed to. Neil and Patricia were married for a total of eight months before they got divorced. Her last straw with him was the day he sent messages to every single one of the guys on her social media accounts and threatened to fight them.

She hadn't even logged into those accounts, but Neil just would never let it go. They fought day and night about it, even though she couldn't even remember her login passwords.

It ate him alive.

And on that day, the day she left on a gray hound bus, he locked her in their apartment and demanded to know every name of any partner she had ever had in the past.

When she told him he was psychotic for acting like this, he picked up a lamp and threw it at her. She ducked and it hit the wall behind her. She began screaming a high pitch scream and banged on the walls so other tenants would hear. She knew how to get help.

This wasn't her first rodeo.

A friendly neighbor called the cops and when they arrived, she took off. She pressed charges on him and served him divorce papers as he sat in the jail cell. It was a quick ordeal because the cops helped her go the fastest route possible and with her pressing charges on him, he wasn't able to fight back in the divorce.

He just had to sign the papers and move on with his life. Even though it was only an eight-month marriage, she was damn glad to be out of sight out and of mind from Neil.

In the divorce she was granted to keep the apartment, but she didn't want him to know where she would be living at, so she politely declined and got the fuck out of there.

*** 

"And you dropped it in the parking lot?" Willow held Neil's phone, looking at the cracked screen, pushing buttons to try to turn it on.

"Yeah, when I got out of the car, I guess I had it on my lap, and boom!" He clapped his hands together. "Smashed right on the concrete." making more hand gestures for even more emphasis.

Willow noticed a gash on his hand. It was a new one. His old ones from hitting the kitchen counter had healed. She asked him about it.

"Oh this?" He held up his hand. "Just an accident. Yeah. I can't even remember how that happened." he hid his hand in his pocket and changed the subject.

Willow knew he was lying. It's not that she knew because he wasn't a good liar. *He was a damn good liar.* She knew because he had already shown his temper before.

# Willow

"We'll see each other soon. I promise. He's starting to let me go places by myself. I have to hold off for just a *little* bit longer. There's no telling when he'll decide to follow me again." Willow sat in her cubicle, texting to Brock.

"It hurts me to read that he *lets* you go places alone. He's controlling you, Willow. I'll fuck him up." Brock said into the talk-to-text mic, then guzzled down whiskey straight out of the bottle as he sat on his couch.

An open box of pizza had been sitting out for days and liquor bottles were littered all over the coffee table in front of him.

"I know. Just be patient with me, okay? It shouldn't be much longer." She quickly texted on the Go Phone Brock bought her just for them to keep in touch. He had snuck it to her one day while she was at work.

He placed it in an envelope and left it with the front receptionist to give to Willow. Nobody had a clue what was going on or who he was. They just thought it was work related. Willow was happy with the results.

She couldn't wait to go to work each day. Not because she loved her job so much. *She did.* But more so because she got to finally have some type of normality and a breather from Neil.

At work she could have any conversation with anybody she wanted, without being asked a million questions. *Who was that? What did they want? Was it a guy?* There was just some things Neil wasn't letting go of.

And questioning her to death was one of them. But at least she could go grab an ice cream cone by herself sometimes. Ice cream was the only thing that settled her stomach. She felt nauseous every day.

On her trips to Braums or the gas station down the road or a pit stop to grab a latte in the morning before work, she'd make every attempt at texting with Brock and he always answered back immediately.

Like he had his phone is in hands already, just waiting for her text every second of the day. Sometimes they'd talk on the phone, just so she could hear the sound of his alluring foreign accent. She was sick of Neil's voice. Even though, once upon a time she loved his foreign accent, too.

She was nervous to tell Brock her fear that she might be pregnant. She, without a doubt knew he would run. But she didn't know who else to talk to about it. The anxiety of a positive showing up, held her back from taking a test. She wasn't independent enough to handle the emotions of taking the test on her own anyway.

Her friends were not the ones to go to about serious situations like this. They were more of the fun kind of friends. The ones you just meet up with a few times a month to chat about the up-and-coming bar, eat sushi with and hear about the new boots they bought online.

They would gossip about friends they each went to high school with and the posts they put out for all the world to see. *"Pray for my boy. He has a scrape on his knee."* or *"Buy my Herbalife and let me change YOUR life"*.

They laughed together about it all. It was a good little escape from reality, hanging with her girls. But that's all she really took it as with them. They didn't know about her marital issues with Neil *or* that he hated them. She never told them anything at all about Brock, even though she knew they'd love a good gossip, and for a few meet-ups the spotlight would be on her seductive affair.

They didn't even know Brock existed. She didn't trust them enough to keep her secret. She could picture Bridgett, the alpha of the group, showing up unannounced at her apartment ready to brawl it out with Neil.

Anna would be supportive enough, but *only* because she was a pervert and would want to hear the juicy sex details and make a joke out of it all. She made everything about sex. And Stacy wouldn't be able to hold back the secret. She'd catch Neil 'accidentally' out and about, and then....

And these are the reasons she never told them about her affair. Which is also the reason she couldn't call them up like friends do for support as she takes a pregnancy test.

*It's definitely time to make more friends.*

For a split second she thought about going to her mom and telling her everything. But Willow knew she'd side with Neil. I mean, not only did the woman not want kids in the first place, but she certainly didn't want a *girl*.

She'd rather have a boy. She was competitive with girls. It was embarrassing watching her compete for Neil's approval. She'd make a huge deal about any small efforts he made. She was almost flirtatious with him.

People on the outside might have thought that. Neil might have too. But Willow knew it was just because of her desperation of wanting a son instead of a daughter, *if she had to have kids*, was causing this annoying schoolgirl-like behavior when they'd go over to their house for dinner once every few months.

Or her parents would come over for Willow and Neil's turn to cook, and he'd want to do it all on his own during those times. His desperation to win her parents approval was just as sickening as her mom's for him.

It didn't matter what he cooked, though. It could be Ramen noodles and when she'd find out that *he* cooked it all on his own, she'd look at him with batty eyes, "Mmmmm. I've never tasted anything so good in my life."

She'd take a big bite out of those sloppy noodles and eat every last drop. Her dad couldn't stand the texture of it and Willow would laugh when he'd say he was just too full from a late lunch. Her mom would elbow him and that was his cue to slurp it all up.

*Yum.*

As for Brock; her sweet, sweet Brock. Willow didn't want to lose him, so she kept her scare of pregnancy in for as long as she could. Until it finally bottled up inside and the big news was about to be blurted out randomly during one of their secret conversations.

# Pauleen

I have a date! A date with my Tillie look-alike, Willow. She offered to have tea and girl talk with me. My daughter never grew into the ages of wanting tea and girl talk, other than when she was five years old and we'd hold tea parties in her playroom.

I soaked those times right up. I was never the mother that would regret not spending enough time with my kid before it was too late. She was my only child. I had all the time in the world for her.

Today, I would get out of my nightgown and wear one of my dresses suited for such an occasion like this. I knew just what to wear! I searched in my closet for the dress, and then I remembered how many actual outfits I have.

I thought of wearing them more often, but my nightgowns were far more comfortable. I found the dress I was looking for hidden in the back with a zipper bag over it. I unzipped the bag and I was met with the sequins of flowers sewn all around the collar.

It was a boat neck dress and reached just under my knees. It was beige and beautiful and I would look like a mother again. I took it out of the bag and dusted it off, then took a lint roller to it just in case anything was left behind. I wanted to look perfect.

I tried it on and when I pulled the zipper up the side, it stopped just before my bust and wouldn't go any further. I sucked in my stomach and continued pulling and tugging at the zipper, and heard a rip. I let out the air I'd been holding in and sullenly took off the dress. I hung it back up because I planned on losing some weight to fit into that beauty again one day.

I searched around my hung-up clothes again for another dress to wear and there was nothing quite as perfect as the one I had just tried on. I settle for a purple one that reached the ground and had black flowers covering the front and back, from the sleeves to the bottom of the dress. When I put this one on, I was happy to see that it actually fit me. It used to be a little loose on me, but now it fits just right.

I had found the perfect little black sandals to match and thought of how Willow would appreciate the floral and sandals because it's what she wore a lot during this time of the year.

The softness of my makeup brushes felt smooth against my skin as I painted my face just a little bit to feel like a woman. I combed through my hair some and stacked it on top of my head in a bun. I used at least twenty bobby pins to get it just right.

Gazing at myself in the mirror, I was quite smitten with the way I looked. I cleaned up quite well, if I do say so myself.

# Brock

My feelings for Willow were stronger than anyone I had ever been with before. It wasn't just the sex, although that certainly helped. But she was kind, with pure eyes and more empathetic than anyone I had ever met before.

She forgave me for decisions I made, like quitting my job without notice. Nobody else would have forgiven me for quitting my job without a backup plan. My day manager was pissed about me leaving without notice and we *really* got into it.

But she forgave me because she knew how long I stuck it out with them. She empathized with me because she could relate to working under assholes who don't appreciate you. I liked working there. I really did.

But people are shit and it's hard to get along with them. If I could find a job that would let me work completely solo, and only join limited conversations with my boss, that would be perfect. Actually, I'd just rather be my *own* boss.

People can *really* piss off.

\*\*\*

"Hey you." Willow breathed into the phone.

"Man. It's so good to hear your voice, even though we just talked yesterday." Brock laughed, rubbing his hands through his hair, letting it fall perfectly back into place.

"I think it's been long enough. I can't take it any longer, Brock. I need to see you." She hid in the bathroom at work for a five-minute break. The chomps of a granola bar Willow ate, crunched in Brock's ear.

Sitting up quickly from his bed, he stumbled getting dressed and balancing the phone at the same time. "Okay. When?"

"I'm taking the rest of the day off work, but I'll need you to pick me up. My car will have to stay here. I can walk down the road to the Valero and meet you there. Afterwards, you can take me back to my car at three-thirty. That way I can just go straight from *'work'* to home. And Neil will never find out."

"Meet you in thirty minutes?" He spread toothpaste on his toothbrush.

*Gotta wash out all the whisky taste.*

"Yeah," her voice was soft. "Yeah. I'd like that." and he could tell she was smiling through the phone.

After Brock got all cleaned up and ready to pick up Willow, he prepared his place for the date he was finally about to get with her again. He tossed away all the trash he let linger across the living room and noticed that it completely overflowed his trash can.

He lit candles in each room of the house and even sprayed his cologne behind the fans after he turned them on to circulate some air. He wiped down all the services of tables and counter tops and tossed his dirty clothes in the washer to start a load. He grabbed a few things he had bought from Home Depot and built a little surprise for Willow in his bedroom.

On his way to pick up Willow from the Velaro down the road from her office, he tossed all the trash in the dumpster and sprayed his car with his cologne to get rid of any lingering smell.

***

Willow hadn't taken not even one sip of alcohol since she suspected she might be pregnant. This day was different, though. First of all, she knew the plans were for her to get an abortion.

She just needed Brock's support *and money* to go through with it. But she first needed to find out if she even *was* pregnant. And second of all, she thought a few sips of liquor wouldn't hurt should she have a sudden change of heart and keep the baby.

The talk with Brock would be hard, or maybe it wouldn't. She really wasn't too sure. Either way, she wanted to prepare for the worst. At the Velero, she bought a home pregnancy test and a bottle of Dr. Pepper.

She hid the test in a zipper pocket in her bag, then poured out half of her drink and filled the rest up with vodka from the stash she keeps in her purse.

*** 

The aroma of her hair was subtle and sweet like honey. I breathed her in completely when she wrapped her arms around me during our first hug in nearly two months. God. I could stay holding her forever.

Things were a little different then, and instead of putting a show on the television to watch and snuggle up together, we just clung to each other like it would be our last date.

Because the reality was, she could leave me that day and I wouldn't be able to see her again for another two months or longer, *or never again.* We had so much time to hang out that day.

I picked her up at eight-thirty in the morning, and didn't have to drop her off until three-thirty in the afternoon. But it was still not enough time with her. I could spend every waking moment with her if she'd let me. If she'd leave that bitch ass husband of hers.

*** 

"So, I take it Neil hasn't suspected anything about the Go Phone yet?" He lit a joint that hung out of her mouth. "Breathe in, girl."

She deeply inhaled, "Nah. He doesn't have a clue." as she exhaled, she threw a coughing fit, then laughed and grabbed her Vodka Dr. Pepper bottle off the coffee table.

"What's it going to take for him to *want* to leave you?" He took a big hit off the joint. "I mean, how many clues does he need? Ya know? Like, hey asshole go fuck yourself and leave us alone." He passed the joint to her.

She put her hand up, "No thank you. I think I'm blitzed already." And pretty soon she fell asleep, sitting upright on his couch.

Brock took her phone that sat on the coffee table and sent Neil a text message: *"I'm sorry to do this through text, but I'm leaving you. I just can't do this any longer. I'm out of state. Don't try to find me because you won't be able to. Goodbye for good."*

He watched her phone light up with a phone call from Neil, and sent him to voicemail. Before shutting the power off to her phone, he

97

called her cell service provider that showed on the phone screen and he pretended to be Willow's husband.

He first requested the GPS tracking be turned off, then took her off his phone plan. Afterwards, he took the battery out of her phone and threw it in one trash can and her phone in another.

Brock grabbed for the morphine off his desk and injected just enough in her arm for a night's sleep.

# Willow

Stretching after a long nap, Willow looked around to see she was then in Brock's bedroom. She assumed that in her drunk and high state that they couldn't keep their hands off each other and ended up in there.

But she didn't see Brock lying beside her in bed. She wondered what time it was. She knew she had to be back at the office at three-thirty. She reached over to grab her phone that she normally set on the nightstand when visiting.

Her hand felt heavy and the unexpected sound of clanking metal pieces struck, one against the other. Sitting up quickly, she saw long chains wrapped around her wrists and ankles.

She followed her eyes to the shackles that linked, and noticed them combined together, and welded unyielding around a metal hook anchored to the ceiling like the eye of a needle, only much bigger, with a lock secured tightly. She thought this was a joke.

*It's gotta be a joke. Maybe he's into bondage? Maybe he's just playing some fucked-up joke on me. Tasteless, sure. But this has to be a joke.*

She called out his name and nothing returned other than her echo. She yanked a chain, making a loud noise when it dropped out of her hands to the floor. When she saw the bedroom window had been boarded up with wood and not a speck of light got in, she realized right then that this was definitely no joke.

She scratched at the wood that covered the window, tried pulling the nails out, and banged against it to the outside world.

"HELP ME!"

A splinter pierced her finger, and she sucked on it, then in a fit of rage she began throwing everything from the nightstand against the amour in front of the bed. A lamp shattered to the floor. Little gold earrings she left there before got lost behind furniture as she threw them.

"You mother fucker! Brock! What the fuck! Brock! Brock! Get me out of these fucking chains right the fuck now!" pulling at all the shackles and letting them drop to the floor to make that loud noise again.

She did this over and over. But Brock didn't return for hours and her voice grew hoarse from yelling out '*help*' more times than she could count, hoping someone might hear her and she'd be let free.

She fell back to sleep out of boredom and pure exhaustion from pulling on the heavy weighted chains that bounded her. She was awakened by Brock kissing her forehead and sat up quickly, then backed up against the headboard of the bed.

"I brought you dinner." Brock sat a tray of what looked and smelled like home cooked food, but she could tell it was bought from the diner down the road. "You were too busy sleeping during dinner time, so I went out for a bit."

She blinked at him.

"Oh no, honey. Not that. I wasn't with any other women or anything like that. I went shopping and bought you some new clothes," he walked out of the room and came back in with bags: Nordstrom, Gucci, Prada and Victoria's Secret. "I got you plenty of clothes and undergarments to last for a bit, but of course I'll be having to buy bigger and bigger clothes as you grow."

He handed her the bags one at a time, waiting to watch her to open it up until giving her the next one. "They're mostly comfortable clothes because you'll be hanging around the house anyway." he smiled as if this was an agreement that they had.

Willow grabbed the bag he handed to her, then chunked it across the room. "What the actual *fuck*, Brock?!" holding back tears. "Don't tell me you're planning on keeping me chained up as your *prisoner*!"

"God. No. Willow, no. You're *not* my prisoner." He rubbed her belly. "You're gonna have my baby. You're gonna be my wife."

"How the *fuck* do you know about that?!" She balled her hands in fists and yanked the restraints like she could break free with muscle. "What have you been doing?! Stalking me?! You fucking psycho!"

Brock grabbed his bedroom chair and pulled it close to Willow. He leaned back with his hands crossed behind his head. "When were you going to tell me you're pregnant?"

"I don't even know if I am. You see? You could let me go. We don't *know* that I'm pregnant, Brock. I think this is a *big* misunderstanding."

"When you fell asleep, no, when you *passed out* from drinking and smoking, I went through your bag and saw a pregnancy test." he held up his pointer finger in suggestion of an idea. "And I thought, *yes*, we could be a little family. We could be happy. Don't you see? This is your get out of jail free ticket from Neil. You don't have to be stuck with him anymore."

Tears dripped down her face. "And we still can be happy. But you have to get me out of these chains."

"But then, but *then,* I went through your phone" He stood and shook his head in disbelief. Looked at her like she's filth. "And I found some interesting stuff, Willow. To say the least." He jerked the chain attached to her wrist, and her upper body heaved forward.

"You searched for ways to have a home abortion, for abortion clinics, for prices of abortions. Instead of your search history being full of baby names, you looked up ways to *kill* our baby. How could you?"

"Brock, do you remember telling me you wouldn't want to bring a child into your world?" She watched him lean his head sideways with his lips pursed together and brows creased. Like he was confused. "You *agreed* with me about not wanting kids. I thought we were on the same page." She massaged her temples from the headache she always got after crying.

"Yes. But that was before you came into my life." He sat back down in the chair.

"But you said it *to* me! I had already come along when you said that!" She reached her hands out to grab what Brock held out to her.

Brock handed her the next bag to look through. *Prada.* And again, she threw it across the room, watching it hit the dresser and fall to the floor.

"Stand up." Brock snapped his fingers.

"Fuck you!"

Brock grabbed her by the arm and she stood to her feet.

"Okay, now hold your hands out as far as you can." and she did. "See? You're not just chained to a bed. You can move your arms and legs. It's really not *that* bad, Willow."

She gritted her teeth and spit on his face. He wiped it away with his shirt and didn't seem bothered.

"Now, here hold these." he bent to pick up the chains and placed them into her arms. "Walk to the furthest you can get around."

She walked to the bathroom in his bedroom, to the shower and toilet. She took a tour to the hallway and was yanked backwards by the chains. She stood in front of a mini refrigerator she hadn't noticed there before.

"This will be your life now. And I think it's pretty lenient given your recent actions, but if you keep declining my gifts and efforts, I'm going to have to shorten that chain, girl."

She began hyperventilating with tears rolling down her face and snot pouring out of her nose. She begged him. "Please don't do this, Brock. Please. I'll keep the baby. I'll do whatever you want. You don't have to keep me chained up like this. I'm yours without all this." flailing her arms around in the air, not being able to stop herself from concentrating on the sounds of the shackles clicking and dragging.

"Only time will tell." Brock walked into the living room. He turned on a comedy movie and Willow could hear him laughing from the other room. She dropped to the floor and pleaded to be let free. Brock propped his legs up on the ottoman and turned the volume to the television up to drown out her sobs.

# Neil

"Yes, officer. Her car is still parked at work, so her text message just doesn't make any sense." Neil held up his phone to the policeman. "And now it's just off. Her phone is *off*. It's Disconnected. I didn't disconnect it."

"And it's been less than twenty-four hours that she left?" the policeman picked at a hangnail.

"She didn't *leave*. She's missing. Something happened to her!" Neil gritted his teeth and said this louder than he meant to.

The policeman looked up at him from the tone in his voice. "You and the Missus ever fight?"

"What?! No! Come on, man! She's missing. I'm telling you right now. She wouldn't take off like this. She never has."

"Well, son, people leave their spouses all the time. Just like this, actually." Crossing his arms together; he glared at him over the ridge of his glasses. He was a heavy-set man and the buttons on his uniform shirt were nearly popping off as he stayed seated in his chair on the other side of the glass from Neil.

He had a widow's peak and other spots of his light-colored hair were balding. But his arms were covered with enough hair to fill in all the bald spots on his head, and then some.

"Okay. And I get that. But her *car* is still at her office. And if you think she'd leave me. Okay, fine let's go with that. But the woman *loves* her job. She wouldn't leave *that* behind. And again, where would she go without her car?"

*Now the mother fucker was filing his nails.*

"I've seen more things people leave behind than a job and a husband."

"And a car?" Neil asked with annoyance and sarcasm in his voice.

The policeman stopped filing his nails and sighed, then gave him a look like he's stupid and this is all irrelevant. "Yes, people leave cars behind all the time when they leave their spouses."

"So, you won't help me? I'm telling you my wife is missing. She didn't just leave me, her job and her car behind. Something is wrong."

He was then biting his nail, and with creased brows he looked at the hang nail he'd been messing with throughout the entire conversation they had.

Neil stared at him with his eyes growing wider and angrier by the second. He snapped his fingers in front of the police officer's face through the square opening of the glass. "He-fucking-llo!" Neil called out to him.

He sighed. "Come back when you have a real missing person's case. Right now, she's just another unhappy wife who left her husband."

"Well, you're a lot of fucking help. Aren't ya?" marching away, he reached for the missing person's posters hung on a dedicated wall, and vigorously tore a few off. "Thanks a fucking lot, asshole!"

***

Neil parked, and '*shit*' he pulled up right beside Pauleen. She hopped out of her car quickly and tapped on his driver's side window.

Neil rolled down his window. "Hi Pauleen. What's up?"

He leaned his head against the seat and looked straight ahead. He clenched his jaw. The thought of having to talk to her right at that moment just pissed him off.

"Where's Willow? We were supposed to have tea and girl talk." she shook her hips a little to show excitement, and smiled real, big and cheesy. She was still all glammed up for the occasion.

"I don't know where she's at." and it just came out like word-vomit "She's missing, Pauleen." He slammed his hand on the steering wheel. "She's fucking *missing*!"

Holding her hand over her heart, her eyes widened "Oh no. Oh dear." She clasped the top part of her dress to show a heart break. "Did you call the cops?"

"What the *fuck* do you think?" his eyes shot daggers at her from the stupid question she had just asked.

"Of course, you did, honey. Of course, you did." She bowed her head to him. "Please keep me updated. I'll join in on any searches. I may be old and semi handicapped, but I got some strength in me for that poor sweet Willow."

"Look. Sorry for snapping at you. It's just been a long day and I'm stressed." He half smiled at her.

"Oh, don't you worry about my feelings, dear. I'd be one mad woman if something happened to my husband." And she carried on the story of how he and Tillie died from a drunk driving accident.

Neil listened only to keep his mind off Willow for at least just a second. Then he told her good night and went into his apartment alone. Now *he* was the one with the lonely flat.

# Pauleen

With my head hanging low, I headed back into my apartment. *I can't lose a daughter again.* Every mother's worst nightmare went through my mind as I undressed and put my nightgown back on.

I slipped on my comfortable slippers and reclined my chair to lean back because my body was aching from all this stress. I reached for the pill bottle on my little table beside my chair and popped *five* Xanax at once. I needed a little extra boost this time because I just didn't know what else to do right then.

The thought of Neil hurting Willow literally made my heart sink to the pit of my stomach. It was not so far-fetched. I could see him killing her and disposing her body like she's trash.

Because to him, she was a possession, not a human being he respected. Would he get away with this? I would make damn sure he didn't. The drunk driver didn't get off so easy when he killed my daughter, Tillie. Neil wouldn't stand a chance if I had anything to do with this.

And I will. I promise you, I will.

# Willow

Eating cheese and grapes, then washing it down with orange juice, Willow stroke up a conversation with Brock. "So, when did you change your mind about wanting a baby? This all just came out of left field to me. Don't be surprised that I hate you now."

He sat in his bedroom chair, facing towards her as she sat up in the bed against the headboard. "When I realized that *you* were the one that could change that for me."

Gulping down the rest of the orange juice in her cup and wiping her mouth with the back of her hand, she pressed on. "And when did that moment happen?"

He looked at his watch. "Hey. I gotta go, but I'll be back in a bit." walking out the bedroom, Brock stopped and didn't turn around "Also, if you scream, nobody can hear you out here. The townhouse beside us is vacant and a lot of old folks live here. They don't get out much, and they're hard at hearing anyway, so I advise you not to try."

He left and when the front door shut, she chunked the empty orange juice glass against the wall. Watching the glass shatter to the floor became one of her favorite hobbies and sounds. "Fuck you, Brock!"

***

I had been there for three full days now, and it was the longest three days of my entire life. It's weird how when you watch movies of the girl being held captive by a psychopath *like Brock* you always think of what you'd do to set yourself free. You yell at the television, giving the girl in chains advice that, well, that is just not plausible when you're actually *in* the situation yourself.

You think *oh, that'll never happen to me. And if it did, I'd find a way out of there. I wouldn't lose hope so quickly.*

Three full days and nights of living hell. Brock wasn't hitting me. He wasn't raping me. He wasn't withholding food or drink from me. And he wasn't even yelling at me.

There are other forms of abuse; ones that are so hard to explain. Like manipulation or that grateful feeling I got when he cooked up a delicious meal. I didn't want to feel grateful for anything he did.

Things could have always been worse, I suppose. But the fact remains that he was holding me captive. He had taken away my freedom. I felt trapped with Neil, but I *was actually* trapped with Brock. I didn't think he saw it that way, and that's what scared me the most. His sense of reality was blurred lines. He *actually* thought he was doing me a favor.

"I'm doing this for you, too."

"How so?"

"I saved you from Neil."

And now I had wished someone would save me from Brock. Maybe even Neil. Because at least with him, it was more of my own self holding me captive. I stayed to not disappoint my mom *again,* to not have to hear my friends say '*I told you so'* because they were totally against me marrying him so quickly.

I didn't want to deal with the drama of leaving Neil, so I dealt with the drama of staying with him. But deep down, I knew he'd let me go. He might have fought me about it, things may have gotten out of control and possibly even worse than what they were.

But not like *this.*

*** 

I started to lose count of the days I had been Brock's prisoner, so I began using a pen from his desk and underneath it, I drew tally marks to keep track. I had been there for twenty-two days then. I could tell by the light and dark beaming through the hallways from windows just out of my reach.

Strange.

It felt like years. I guess that's how slow time passes when you have no form of entertainment of your choice. Brock would sometimes put on a DVD through his computer that sat on the desk in his room. That was my only escape.

I'd dream of myself as Dorothy from Wizard of Oz that he played for me over and over. I would follow the yellow brick road back to home. I'd always get lost, but the Wizard would grant my wish and shoot me into the sky, and the sunlight felt good on my skin.

The breeze in the air swayed through my hair. Then I'd be back in my own living room, free to wander around any room I wanted. I could drive in my car to grab a latte and head back into work.

My coworkers would praise me for being so strong and coming back to work right away. And my boss would pay me to write about my experience. But that all faded away every time I woke up, because I was stuck there for who knew how long.

I wondered if my mom was looking for me. And I wondered if there was a missing person's report on me. I would daydream of signs with a picture of my face stapled to trees, poles, hung in windows.

*Have you seen her?*

I had nothing but my thoughts in this lonely room. I had stopped yelling for help because the last time I did, Brock came home early and heard me. He followed through with his promise; the chain was indeed shortened. I had to ask him to go to the bathroom and bring me food for days.

I'd do anything to keep as little communication as possible with him. So, I kept quiet even after he left for however long he'd be gone some days. I had learned my lesson the hard way.

\*\*\*

Dancing around in his boxers, Brock said he had good news. It had surpassed the deadline of a legal abortion and he was happy because he would get to keep his *'family'*. He unlocked all the chains wrapped around me and told me I was free to join him in the living room for a movie night.

*A celebration* he called it.

Rubbing my wrists and ankles like an inmate in jail who just got their cuffs off, I sat down on the opposite side of the couch as him.

"I thought we'd snuggle. Ya know? For old times' sake." He held his hand out towards me.

I looked down and fiddled with my thumbs, "I just—"

He sighed. "Do you need to go back to the chains?"

I slid over towards him.

"I love this show. You ever watch How I Met Your Mother?" Brock looked at the television with a big cheesy grin.

"Yeah." I only gave one worded answers if I could help it.

Lighting up a joint, he inhaled deeply, then let out a coughing laugh. "Here" he passed the joint to me. And I thought about this for a minute. This was my opportunity to gain his trust, hopefully be let free from the chains more often.

"No thank you." I smiled at him and rubbed my belly.

"See? I *knew* you'd be a good mom." He inhaled a big drag and laughed at a part of the show that I didn't find any humor in.

\*\*\*

It's now day thirty-three. I'd been there for over a month. I wanted to watch cable T.V. I needed to see if my face was in the front and center of the missing people. I had a plan.

When Brock got home, I'd sweet talk him into letting me watch live cable television in the living room. He started to trust me more and more. I was freed from the shackles a few times a week then.

Every little trust I gained in him, flirty look I gave, laugh I forced out, *Mmmm* sound I made at his cooking was all just a ploy to get to my freedom.

*I can play games, too. You son of a bitch.*

"You know, I was thinking we could watch some cable tonight. I'd love to eat dinner with you in the living room. Ya know, prepare for our baby seeing what an at home date could look like. Can we? Please?"

Twirling my hair, I flashed that pretty smile he loved to see.

"Sure. Yeah. Of course." he gathered up dinner trays and pulled out meat to thaw. "I'll unchain you when it's all ready for us." he yelled out to me from the kitchen. Then gliding to the bedroom, I lay in, he stood at the doorway and flashed a smile at me like we were going on a real date or something.

"I was kind of thinking I could help you cook tonight. Don't you think that'd be romantic?" still twirling my hair, gazing into his eyes.

The temptation was almost too much for him to say no, but thinking of the knives on the kitchen counter and any other item that could be used as a weapon; he told me another time would be better.

*** 

I'd finally almost gained his complete trust. It was now fifty-three days stuck in there with this psychopath. My stress levels were through the roof, but around him I kept calm. I wanted him to think I was happy where I was at. So, I played along with his little mind fuck games, and fell closer to freedom each time I passed his test.

*** 

Brock chopped potatoes on the cutting board in the kitchen. "I feel like you've been a really good wife here lately, Willow."

She sat on the couch in her Victoria Secret pajama set he bought for her. Even in pregnancy she was tiny. Barely a bump would show. "I have?!" forcing excitement out.

*Good. My plan is working.*

"Yes. How would you feel about staying unchained from now on when I'm home and awake?" The chopping stopped and he gazed at her. "That is, of course, you can be a good girl?"

She kneeled on the couch with her hands together like she was praying, "Please. Yes. I'll be good. I promise."

"Because, one thing. That's all it takes. And you're back in the chains." slicing the potatoes again. "Understood?"

"Understood." and she saluted him.

# Neil

It had been two months since my wife went missing. Her parents and friends, my parents, and I all went to the police station together. We protested outside three weeks after they declined my advances before. When passer-by's heard about the story, they joined right in with us. And pretty soon hundreds of people were out there holding up their decorated signs and demanding justice for Willow.

The police station finally gave in, and a missing person's report was sent all over social media. A news station even covered the story, asking for anyone who had *any* information to call the hotline number at the bottom of the screen. More missing posters and signs were hung around *three* states.

All those protests, showing her picture, having sobbing parents and a concerned husband really helped build this up. Thousands of people from all over joined in the search parties.

Carnivore dogs picked up no sense of her, except for one the second time they came out. They strolled along and stopped at the Valero down the road from her work. After that, nothing was ever picked up from the dogs again. They pulled the cameras from the Valero and saw her walking on the sidewalk.

She kept on walking where the cameras didn't pick up and the carnivore dogs picked up her last scent on that sidewalk.

People didn't stop searching though. They cleared out bodies of water, and asked around at pubs, coffee shops, book clubs, and grocery stores showing her pictures to workers and people walking the streets.

Most of them glanced at her picture and said "no" quickly, then headed off to wherever they were in a hurry to get to. Still, despite all our efforts nobody came close to finding her. And to gain more publicity in hopes of finding her, dead or alive, the story became international news.

*The beautiful blonde from Chicago finally made that headline news.*

\*\*\*

A ding came through Neil's phone and to his surprise the ex's, Claudia and Patricia had invited him to a group chat on Facebook. Curiously, he clicked the accept button and read on to their accusations.

Claudia: "Hey asshole. What did you do to her?"

Patricia: "Yeah. Asshole! Finally snap and kill this one?"

*Wow. So, they haven't changed at all. Bitches.*

He replied back, "Fuck off!" and then shut his phone off.

\*\*\*

Neil had been divorced from Patricia for two months before he met Claudia. They met at the college he transferred to for his Associates degree. She was passing through to have a tour of the school and she bumped right into him after she took a drink out of the water fountain that he waited in line behind her for.

They both laughed and she looked down blushing and embarrassed from him noticing the water that had splashed on her shirt. She walked off and headed back to the Dean giving her the tour and turned to look at Neil who had been checking her out. She smiled and looked down again. He liked to see her blush like that.

He found her even more beautiful than Patricia. He also thought about how she could be the woman to help him get over the loss of Patricia. He was still searching for her day and night online, even though they'd already signed the divorce papers.

He was still fixated on understanding why she wanted to leave him *and how dare she.* But Claudia's beauty and brains made him forget all about Patricia that day. He knew a woman who was getting a tour at the college would be better for him than some stripper who couldn't stay away from other guys.

Claudia had medium length auburn red hair, that was clearly not her natural hair color but it really favored her olive skin tone. Her eyes were green and would sometimes change to blue depending on her mood.

When she was down or clam, they were blue. When she was hyper or angry, they were green. She was top heavy and thick on the bottom, too. She was skinny in the places it mattered to him, like her stomach, legs, arms and neck. She was fit.

She worked out and would wear yoga pants and t-shirts as her main wardrobe. Neil absolutely lusted over her every day, as many men did that she crossed paths with.

Claudia and Neil exchanged numbers the second time he ran into her at the college. This time, she had gone to sign paperwork to complete classes online. She was also going for an Associate's degree.

Neil and Claudia would meet in separate cars to go on dates and tried out many different restaurants that were between their apartments, so they could meet in the middle.

He treated her like royalty on their dates and would wink at her from across the table. She never had to open a door when she was with him or pull out her own chair or pay for any meal or any drinks when they went out.

Their dates continued on like this for five months and on one of those dates, he dropped to one knee and proposed to her as the table was covered in rose peddles, with the ring in a box that was hidden under her napkin.

She squealed and said yes with happy tears springing to her eyes. Two weeks later they were married. Another Justice of the Peace wedding, just like with Patricia. They had eloped and didn't tell their family until after they got back from the beach for their honeymoon.

He took Claudia a little more seriously than Patricia. His honeymoon with Patricia was locking the doors to their apartment and shutting their phones off for a week. When it came to Claudia, he was smitten and in love.

Once they got back from their honeymoon, he had asked her to drop out of college. She wasn't too thrilled about this request and of course told him no. She had dreams, too.

She wanted to be somebody, too. She wanted a career, too. She even tried helping him to understand that all her classes were online, so it wasn't like she couldn't give him enough of her time.

He tried explaining to her that she didn't really need college now that she was a married woman. They'd argue about it frequently and it was the first red flag she noticed. But she was a calm woman and always tried reasoning with him when he'd throw a fit.

117

One of those fits were about her yoga pants being too tight. She couldn't understand why he all the sudden needed her to change so much about herself, when all of the things he had asked her to change were what she was when she first met him. She started to wear shirts that covered her ass to not upset him so much when they'd go out in public. He slowly but surely tore her self-esteem down one day at a time.

Neil's mother and her own mother began seeing the signs and tried helping her. Neil's mom would hear it in her voice when she'd call or see them on video chat. They lived out of state.

She had begun giving her advice, but got quiet as a mouse once she heard Neil coming home or passing through the room that they chatted in. Claudia's mother asked her to divorce him and come move back home with her and her husband. She even set up a room for her there.

She could tell her daughter was disappearing and basically half dead. Claudia did feel like she loved him and was devoted to him. But she wasn't too far gone that she couldn't see the changes within herself.

She knew he was tearing her apart. She always tried to please him and keep him calm, however when they went out on dates for some reason after they got married his temper would become out of control about men gawking at her. She was a beautiful woman.

It didn't matter if her shirt covered her back side or cleavage, she was going to be looked at. Neil couldn't stand it. The day she knew she had to go was when he took things a little too far.

They had been married for one year at this point and Neil requested that she stop wearing makeup and dying her hair. He told her she looked like she was asking for it when she painted her face like a whore and colored her hair an unnatural color. The words were painful and she knew she needed to get out.

She called his mother and began crying. She had hoped this would be what could make him stop the verbal abuse and control. Neil's mother told her about his previous marriage and this is what gave her the courage and strength to ask for a divorce. She called her mom and told her all that had been going on, all the secrets of Neil's abusive and controlling ways and his previous divorce, that she had no clue about.

When Neil came home from work, both of her parents and her were sitting in the living room with all of his stuff packed up. Claudia felt confident and held her head high. She wore extra makeup that day and tied her shirt up to the side to show the curve of her ass in the tightest yoga pants she owned.

Neil was kicked to the curb and the divorce papers were served immediately. He moved to a different state, just like he did after his divorce from Patricia, even though he had moved back once he felt like enough time had passed. Plus, it's where Willow really wanted to live.

He decided from now on, he would only date women whose parents weren't so involved in their daughter's life.

***

Neil hadn't slept in days. Passing out on the couch like he had since Willow went missing, he woke up in a cold sweat from a dream of his wife asking him for help. She held out her hand and told him to follow her.

Then led him to a riverbank and said she'd been thrown over. She told him her body was wilting away under water.

***

"Have you guys checked the rivers?" Neil asked the same policeman at the front desk, who paid too much attention to his nails last time.

"Yes sir!" He gave him his full attention this time.

"All of them?" Neil leaned over the counter, crossing his forearms.

"All of them meaning?" his brows furrowed.

"I know of the three you guys drained, but there are many, many more. What if she's." And he didn't finish. He assumed the policeman caught his drift.

"Well, some of them we just can't drain. It could take months to a year. Possibly longer than a year."

"So, what are you waiting on? Time is a tickin." Neil tapped his watch.

"It's not that easy, sir." He stood from his chair. "But I can get you the Chief of the unit here and see what we can do for you."

"Thanks. I'd appreciate that." He made nervous tapping sounds on the counter as he waited to be seen. He realized it might take a

119

while, so he took a seat in the lobby area right across from the guy's desk he was just talking to.

He noticed a woman close to his age crisscrossing her hands anxiously. And he thought she had been told the same thing and wondered who she was looking for. Was it her daughter? Her mother?

*Sit here. Wait. Hopefully her skull isn't broken into a million pieces. Hopefully she's not lying dead in a ditch somewhere. Yes. Sit here. Wait.*

A man older than dirt came out and introduced himself. *Great. He probably doesn't even remember what he does for a living.*

"Chief Phills the name." He shook Neil's hand. *What a grip. Okay, maybe he's still got that fight in him.*

Popping a peppermint in his mouth, he offered one to Neil. Neil put up his hand and thanked him anyway. "Alright. Follow me then and we'll get ya all set up."

Posters of missing persons covered the walls, dates caught Neil's eyes when some of these women hadn't been found for going on twenty years. Anxiety and fear crept and crawled through him, leaving him lightheaded and a bit disoriented when he finally took a seat on the other side of the chief's desk.

Chief Phill crossed his legs. "So what can I do ya for?" *see, grandpas talk like that. God. I'll never say that line again.*

"It's my understanding that you've been able to drain three bodies of water in search of my wife, Willow, and words can't even express my gratitude. But I'm wondering if you've checked *all the rivers.*"

Chief Phill rubbed his chin and looked up to the ceiling in confusion then back at him, "What do you mean by *all the rivers?*"

"Well, I guess I just feel that because there *are* so many rivers around here, within even a few hundred-mile radius, that we could check them all." he leaned in closer to the chief.

"I see. Some of the rivers could take months, even up to a year to drain, and some of them we just don't have in our budget." He rocked back and forth a little in his rolling chair. It made a squeaking sound.

Chief Phill looked to be close to his retirement age. He was lean, but with a bit of muscles showing through his arms, a few tattoos too. He had a thick mustache that was the same salt and pepper color as his hair, and his tan looked like it came from a weekly tanning bed visit.

"Yes sir. I understand. But what can we do to get closer to at least checking *some* of them out?"

Chief Phill made a sucking sound on his peppermint, "Can I ask what your fascination with rivers are? I mean, we could be checking more wooded areas within a few hundred-mile radius." leaning in close to make eye contact. "So... why rivers?"

"With all due respect, sir. If we can be checking out wooded areas within a few hundred-mile radius I'd like to get on that asap." looking down, he sighed and crossed his hands together. "I had a dream."

"What kind of a dream?" And the sound in his voice didn't sound condescending, so Neil looked up to meet his eyes.

"My wife led me to a bridge over a river and pointed to the water. She said that's where she's at." He shifted in his seat. "And I just thought.... hell, I don't know what I thought. I guess I thought that maybe she's giving me answers in my sleep."

Uncrossing his legs, Chief Phill slid his chair up to the desk and handed out a business card. "I don't think you sound crazy. Now, I will say that I don't usually use people's dreams as evidence in a case, but I want you to contact me if anything else happens."

Neil grabbed the business card from Chief Phill's hand, "Thank you. I appreciate that. But is there something we can do right now?"

"We're doing all we can and will not rest until we bring your wife back home." Chief Phill stood from the desk.

"I'll be in touch, Chief Phill. Thanks for your time." he shook his hand.

"You betcha."

When Neil walked out of his office, Chief Phill leaned back in his chair and rubbed his chin again. He thought it was a little strange that he asked specifically about rivers. He suspected the husband had something to do with Willow's disappearance and began looking up Neil's history online.

***

Since his dream of Willow, Neil would park and watch Brock come and go at his fancy town home complex some days. There were no signs of Willow to his knowledge.

Still, he persisted on stalking him every now and then just to see if there were any signs that he had killed her. He drove slowly and far enough behind him to see if he would revisit the riverbank that he

121

possibly dumped her body in. But Brock didn't ever stop at any bodies of water.

He did normal things like going grocery shopping, stopping in a drive through, and buying building materials at Home Depot. Nothing depicted he was guilty of the crime or of any crime for that matter.

This confused Neil, and while he originally didn't think to give his name to the officers in charge of her case, he thought of doing so then.

On his way back to the police station to give them Brock's name, he pulled over to the side of the road. Rubbing his temples from a headache caving in, he thought of confronting Brock instead of allowing the police to take their sweet ass time.

He visualized how the conversation would go. He pictured punching Brock in the face as soon as he opened his door. He wondered why he hadn't seen him at any search parties, but only one.

*Maybe he was too busy? Maybe he just didn't care anymore because Willow broke it off with him months ago?*

He knew he had to gather his thoughts and be precise should he knock on Brock's door. He noticed Brock didn't get any visitors, and thought possibly his family lives out of state, or maybe he was just a loner. Curiosity killed the cat.

Neil wanted to talk to him and ask him for any clues. So, he gathered his thoughts before making his way over. He didn't know what he'd say or do when face to face with him. He had to come up with a plan first. He pulled a notepad and pen out of the glove compartment of his car and began taking notes so he wouldn't freeze when he got there.

He scribbled through all the notes he took and wrote *Kill the bastard*. Then put the notepad back in the glove compartment. His phone rang and he looked to see that it was Chief Phill. He sent him straight to voicemail. He didn't have time to talk. He needed to get busy.

Turning his car back around to go to Brock's town home, he made a little pit stop at a gas station first.

# Brock

Willow lays there with a bump in her belly. That bump is *mine;* she is *mine.* I placed my hand on her stomach to feel any kicks, but it was too soon for that. I was ready to find out the sex.

We wouldn't know until the baby arrives, though. We had planned to do a water birth. I had read up enough about it and learned a lot from my dad. I felt confident in doctoring her throughout this journey of ours'. Willow would be safe.

The baby would be safe. And I'd be medicating her so she wouldn't have to feel the agonizing pain new mothers always have to go through. I would babysit while she slept. I'd go to parenting classes before our child would enter the world; I'd be the best daddy anyone could ever ask for.

Willow seemed to enjoy her time here. I knew she would eventually. I think the shock of waking up shackled like that is what scared her at first. But she lightened up and accepted it, like the good girl she is.

Even in pregnancy she was the most profoundly beautiful woman I had ever laid my eyes on. In fact, it made her more stunning to me. Our baby would grow to be handsome, or pretty with our blood mixed together for sure.

Even though Willow was accepting of her shackles, I couldn't be stupid like Neil was and let her free. She was too destructive and would ruin what we had going for our family.

I'd need to keep her bound for a little while longer. At the point I would see in her eyes that she loves me again, *like I saw before,* is when I would unlock those chains to let her choose her destiny. And I knew when that happened, her choice would be to stay. Everything I did, I did for her.

# Pauleen

"It just doesn't sit well with me" Pauleen said to Chief Phill.

"I see. And when did these incidents start happening?" He leaned in close to her over his desk and studied her body language.

It made her feel nervous. Not because she had done anything wrong, but because a man was looking at her body and she hadn't even been out of her apartment in years.

"It wasn't long after they moved in beside me. The walls are as thin as a toothpick. I can hear everything."

Chief Phill rocked back and forth in his rolling chair and let out a sigh in relief. "Hold on just a second. Okay?"

He turned to the side to face his computer and pulled up Neil's divorce and jail records. He glanced over it to gather names because he didn't have them memorized just yet.

"Have you ever heard the names Patricia or Claudia through the thin walls?"

Pauleen scrunched her face and kept quiet for a second to think back. She wanted to make sure everything she told the Chief was correct and that she wouldn't act on emotion.

Still, she wondered why two other women's names came up in this room when talking about the disappearance of Willow. She wondered if Neil had killed them, too. She wondered if she had been living next to and having conversations with a serial killer. She kept quiet longer than she expected to.

"You alright, there? Do you need some water? Here, let me turn the fan on for you."

She had been sweating profusely since he mentioned Patricia and Claudia. Her hot flashes were in full blast right then.

"Here. Have some water." He handed her a cold bottle of water out of his mini refrigerator.

Pauleen opened the bottle of water, guzzled it down in one sitting and patted her face with the water dripping from the outside of it. "Thank you. I'm sorry."

"You have absolutely nothing to be sorry about. This is a hard situation to bear and from the sounds of it, Willow meant a lot to you."

She froze. "Meant? That's past tense." Tears swelled in her eyes. "Don't tell me you think she's dead."

Chief Phill watched her cry for minute. He let her feel the emotions he knew he could ease with just a few words, but waited for the right time. He needed to talk when she stopped hyperventilating.

He handed her the tissue box and waited for her to ask another question. He knew she would. He had been doing this for thirty years. When she'd ask another question, that's when he could ease her heart a little.

Pauleen blew her nose and grabbed another tissue to blot the tears off her eyes. She took a deep breath and asked for another bottle of water. He grabbed one again from his mini refrigerator and handed it to her. He leaned his back side against the desk and crossed his arms.

"You don't really think she's dead, do you?" Pauleen asked him as she wiped her nose with a tissue.

"No mam, I do not think she's dead. I think Willow means a lot to you. It sounds like you two are close."

"We are. We were supposed to have tea and girl talk before she went missing. I was going to talk her into leaving her husband that day."

Chief Phill cleared his throat and sat back down in his chair. "Do you think she may have already been planning to do that?"

"I don't know." She pulled her shoulders up and her voice cracked. "I don't know. I sure hope so. The thing is, he looked at her like a possession. Like property, not like his wife, his partner or a person. I heard through the walls." She glanced over at his computer screen. "Those girls. What are their names again?"

"Patricia and Claudia" He felt satisfied now that he had them memorized. "Ever heard anything about them?"

"One day I did. It was Claudia. I remember because I thought to myself, *he must be cheating* but then I heard more. He said she changed her last name after they got divorced. It sounded like this was all news to Willow. She was pretty upset about the whole ordeal."

He looked ahead of him, thinking about exactly what he would say when he contacts them. He shook his head back and forth in agreement of his thoughts.

"So, what happened next?"

"I went over there. Willow was acting scared. She had her body hidden behind the door. I couldn't see if she was covered in bruises or not. Dear Lord, I hope not, but I think she was."

Pauleen thought about Willow having an affair. She heard it all through the paper-thin walls. She pondered on the idea of telling Chief Phill about this. Not to throw Willow under the bus, but to incriminate Neil even more.

She thought it to be possible he would have ended up doing something to her based off her cheating on him. She decided not to tell him. They had enough to label him a suspect already. She didn't want to ruin Willow's good name.

"These women, Patricia and Claudia are both his ex-wives. I'm assuming Willow didn't know about Patricia either since only Claudia was brought up. I'll be checking into all of this, and we will bring Willow home." he told her, trying to wrap up the conversation. He had to get busy if he was going to solve this case before Willow was found dead by some fisherman in a faraway swamp land.

Pauleen looked at him with desperation and hope in her eyes. "You promise?"

Chief Phill swallowed hard. He knew if he didn't yes, she would cry again, possibly even have a full-blown melt down. He was good at his job, but he wasn't a counselor.

"No mam. I cannot make any promises. The reason being is because we're taught that from day one of starting this position to not do so. We can't and won't make promises to friends and family of missing persons. But don't lose hope. We're doing all that we can, and we won't stop until we find her."

At his response, Pauleen was silent for half a minute. Chief Phill held his breath and wondered what she might do. She pursed her lips together, then thanked him for his time. She guzzled down some more water, then asked him to walk her out to her car because she felt dizzy and lightheaded.

*\*\**

Today, I got dressed again. The circumstances were sadly not for tea and girl talk with Willow. I had worn my moo, moo, nightgowns every day at home, for years now. I lived in them. The first time I had gotten in regular clothes in years was to impress Willow with tea and girl talk; my way of saving her before she wound up dead at the hands of Neil.

I got dressed in regular clothes again today, and once again it was for Willow. I had hoped that my efforts and information I gave to Chief Phill would be helpful enough for them to start interrogating Neil. I wanted him to go down for all he had done to Willow, and for whatever reason it was that she was missing.

I just knew he had a part in it. I hoped she wasn't dead. I prayed to God every single night to bring her back home alive.

When I got back to my apartment, I of course put on a nightgown. A pastel green one this time, with my matching slippers that have a little bow sewn in at the top. I grabbed the picture of Tillie off the mantel and kicked my slippers off even though I had just put them on.

I walked over to the front door and slid my husband's boots on my feet. They felt rough without socks on, but I didn't care at the time. I just wanted to be close to both of them again.

I reclined in my chair and popped a few of my special pills that I hadn't taken all day. I was too worried about wrecking my car and killing other drivers on the road. The pills had always given me a high feeling, a numbness. Someone had to care about other drivers on the road. I curled into a ball and hugged the picture of Tillie, then cried until I fell asleep.

# Chief Phill

When Chief Phill got done with walking Pauleen to her car and making sure she seemed alright before driving out of the parking lot, he went back into his office to make a few phone calls and gather up some addresses before heading out for a long day and night.

His first phone call was to Neil. After only three rings he heard his voicemail chime in his ears, then left him a message he thought would appeal a same day call back from Neil.

"This is Chief Phill. I've gathered up some new information regarding your wife, Willow's case. I'm hoping you can help me figure some things out. Give me a call back, and let's set up a time for you to come in."

He hung up and rocked back and forth again in his chair. He tried not to suspect him even more for sending him to voicemail so quickly, but after talking with Pauleen, Neil was now his number one suspect and anything he did or didn't do was analyzed by Chief Phill.

He wrote *6/12, 3:43pm, Called Neil, VM after 3 rings,* then he pressed the sticky note on the board behind his desk.

He moved the mouse of his computer screen and was back on the same page he left, the one about Claudia and Patricia. He clicked another tab and searched around for Claudia's information first.

He needed to find an address, a phone number, a social media page, anything that could link him to talking with her. Claudia was fairly easy to find. With just typing her first and last name into a web browser, he found her Facebook, Twitter, Instagram, and a website she had up for the world of yoga lovers to buy her merchandise and join in with her for online and in person classes.

Chief Phill noticed how attractive she was and wondered how in the world this asshole, Neil had gotten so lucky to have been married to two beautiful and successful women. *The lucky bastard.* He clicked a few links on her website and got a phone number to call her direct line.

"Thank you for calling Claudia's Yoga Experience!" She sounded like a cheerleader.

Chief Phill sat up in his seat and cleared his throat. He hadn't expected her to answer so quickly. He thought he might get a voicemail, then he'd have to go searching for her private cell phone number or parents or write her on social media. Not that these were difficult tasks, he just hadn't had much experience finding a past victim of a predator's so easily.

"Hi Claudia. My name is Chief Phill."

She didn't even give Chief Phill another second to waist before chiming in, "Hi Chief Phill! Are you interested in taking my classes or are you calling about purchasing my mats and yoga balls for your at home experience? Either way, you get a free Claudia's Yoga Experience water bottle to go along with *your* yoga experience." She was a natural born saleswoman.

"Actually, I'm calling about something else." He rolled his chair forward and rested an elbow on the desk. "Neil, your ex-husband." He held his breath and squinted his eyes, hoping she wouldn't hang up in his face. He could hear movement in her background.

Her voice went lower, not as chipper as it was when she first answered the phone. "Give me one minute please."

"No problem." He heard a door close on the other end of the line.

"Okay. What about Neil? Who is this again?" Her voice was still low.

"This is Chief Phill. Sorry to call you out of the blue like this. I work on missing persons cases in Chicago. I need to ask you a few questions about Neil, if you don't mind."

"If Neil is missing, I don't know anything about it. We haven't talked since before we got divorced, and that was... oh, like four years ago now. I don't think I can be of any help. I'm sorry."

"Neil isn't missing. His wife is."

Chief Phill knew he wouldn't hear her talk on the other end once he said that. He looked at her picture on the website. She gave a large smile as she posed in warrior position in her yoga outfit that read *Claudia's Yoga Experience* on her top.

The class present for the picture faced towards her in the same position, and they all wore their own colors of her merchandise.

"I-I don't know what to say." She sounded nervous then.

"He doesn't know I'm calling you, so no need to panic. You're safe." Chief Phill listened on for her breath of relief. She released it.

"Okay. Good. Thank you. Please don't tell him you spoke to me. I will help you with whatever you need help with, but I'd rather remain anonymous."

"Not a problem. Can you tell me what your marriage was like to Neil?"

Claudia told him every detail. She hadn't forgotten a thing, even though she had moved on with her life, remarried and even had a two-year-old son now. She couldn't forget, and the thought of another woman marrying Neil and coming up missing scared her.

Not for her own safety, but for Willow's. She told him every gruesome detail of their marriage, how she met him, and when he changed into the monster lurking under your bed.

Chief Phill thanked her and said he'd call her again should he have any more questions.

"Wait!" She was louder than she meant to be. "Sorry. I wanted to ask before we get off the phone. Will you please let me know if she's found alive or—"

She didn't want to say the word dead. She was scared she would manifest Willow's death to the universe.

"Yes, of course. Of course, I will. You take care now." and they both hung up the phone.

Chief Phill went through his recent phone log and dialed Neil again. This time it rang and rang until his voicemail prompted him again. He didn't leave a message. He turned to the sticky note and logged the time he called with how many rings it took to get to voicemail this time.

He turned to his computer screen again and pulled up another tab. He searched for Patricia using the multiple last names in her records. He didn't find a flashy social media account advertising herself, not one that she used recently anyway.

The ones he found were nearly six years old. That's how long it had been since she posted to any of those accounts. He didn't find a home address or phone number, either. He scratched his head and let out a sigh. He searched in her records for her parents, and he did find their contact information.

He called the many numbers they had listed and each of them led him to a voicemail or an answering machine message with other people's names that didn't match Patrcia's parents' names. Some answered and told him he had the wrong number. He continued calling the list of numbers, and when he got to the third from last one, a raspy voice answered.

"Hello?"

"My name is Chief Phill and I'm looking for your daughter, Patricia. Are you, her mother?" He opened up a peppermint and stuck one in his mouth.

"Yes. I'm Patricia's mother. You say you're a Chief of Police? What did she do this time?" The woman had a raspy manly voice, like she had been smoking her whole life.

"No mam." Chief Phill shook his head. "She didn't do anything wrong."

"Then what do you want?" She sounded annoyed.

"I need to ask her a few questions about her ex-husband, Neil."

"She was married before? Huh. Bitch didn't tell me. Can you even imagine? Can you *just* imagine giving up nine months of your body? You can't smoke. You can't drink. Nothing."

"You give up nine full months of your woman-hood and the little chunky baby you push out grows up to be a stripper and a prostitute. Then the bitch doesn't even tell you she got married. I would've gone to the wedding."

The curves of Chief Phill's mouth turned down. He thought of what a retched childhood Patricia must have had growing up with this woman as a *mother* then to get tossed into prostitution, only to be preyed upon by a man who he was sure of had killed his wife.

His heart broke for Patricia and he wondered where she was at. Was she under a bridge, getting into cars with strangers to let them violate her body for a bump? Did she run away, hitch hiking and get picked up by another predator who did worse to her than any other guy could have?

Was she dumped in a river, disposed of like the trash her mother thinks of her, and the world just… forgot? Or did she run off and find her prince charming, get married to the right guy, pop out a few kids and live in a nice home with friendly neighbors who wave to you from their front porches in the morning as she grabs the mail?

He hoped it was the last one.

"Do you happen to know how I can get a hold of her?" Chief Phill asked, hoping she actually had an answer, but doubted she did.

"Don't you think if I knew where she was, I would've already told you? If she's out there, she needs to be put behind bars. That's the only way she'll stay out of trouble or not get herself killed." She chuckled and her smoker's cough came through.

"Please call me if you hear from her. Will you write my number down?"

"Ugh. Hold on and let me get something to write with." Her uncaring attitude pissed off Chief Phill and he rolled his eyes, but didn't say anything about it like he used to with these types of *parents*.

He learned that they were always far too self-centered to give any details to him after he ripped them a new one. He wanted to make sure he didn't ruin an opportunity of getting information about Patricia in the near future.

"Okay. I'm ready. What is it? And please be quick. My show is coming on."

After he gave her the number, he asked if she wanted him to call if he finds her. She hung up on him before he could finish what he was saying.

***

Chief Phill pulled up the tabs on his computer again. He specifically went to the ones of Patricia's social media accounts. He studied each one, analyzing any patterns he might find that would give him a clue to her whereabouts. There were seven Myspace accounts and eight Facebook profiles in her name.

He dug through each Myspace account first, and he noticed that her number one friend on each one was a young woman named Angie. At the time she was more like a kid, a nineteen- or twenty-year-old.

He clicked on Angie's Myspace page and South Park Mexican sang all about a Bloody War. He listened to the song and bobbed his head back and forth a little as he read her about me and skimmed her blogs. He clicked on the send message button and typed a short and straight to the point message.

"*The name is Chief Phill, here. I'm looking for Patricia. She isn't in trouble. Her ex-husband's wife is missing. I need to ask her a few questions. Please send her my way if you know where Patricia is at.*" Then he left a phone number to reach him at.

He copied the message he had sent to her, in case he needed to send it to someone else. Afterwards, he went through each of Patricia's Facebook accounts, and Angie was the first one to pop up on her thread on the first one he went to. She wrote on her page.

*"Girl! Omg! Call me asap!"*

He clicked Angie's profile and noticed that she was an avid poster. She posted about politics, love, true crime, and pictures of her family. She posted several times a day.

He went to her inbox and pasted the same message he had sent her on Myspace and clicked the send button. Chief Phill clicked back on Patricia's Facebook account and sent her a message, too.

*"Patricia, my name is Chief Phill and I'm concerned about the safety and disappearance of Neil's current wife. I just have a few questions to ask you. He won't know a thing. I hope you're safe and doing well. Get back to me. -Chief Phill."*

He copied and pasted this message into every single one of Patricia's social media accounts. He then heated up his half-eaten burger from lunch time and waited for a response. At the same time as the microwave dinged to him that his food was ready, another ding came through the computer.

Angie had written him back.

*"Give me a call. 555-9860"*

Chief Phill left his burger to get cold again and called Angie. His stomach grumbled and was angry at him for the neglect. He had to call her right then. She was online, ready to talk.

He couldn't pass up the opportunity of finding Patricia, for a *burger*. Too many people had let her down and traded her for whatever satisfied them at the time. He needed to talk to her about Willow *and* what lifestyle Patricia was living right then.

"Hello, this is Angie." She sounded professional and motherly at the same time. Her voice reminded him of his mother's when he was a little boy.

"Hi Angie. This is Chief Phill. Thank you for getting back to me so quickly." He gawked at the burger in the microwave, then shut the door and turned his chair around to face his office door.

"Hold on, baby girl. I'll be right back. Can you take her for me? Thanks." Shuffling sounds filled Chief Phill's ears. "Sorry about that. Had to pass my little girl off to her daddy."

"No worries." he waved his hand in the air, like they were talking in person. "I don't mean to sound like a jack ass, but I need to get straight to the point because time is of the essence right now. Do you know where Patricia is or how I can get a hold of her?"

"Patricia doesn't want to be found, but I think under this circumstance, with her identity under lock and key, she'd help. That's why I gave you, my number. I'm the only one from her past that she's still in cahoots with."

"How can I get a hold of her?" he was relieved to hear she was alive.

"Let me call her and ask if it's okay that I give you her number. I'll call you back."

After they got off the phone, he pulled his burger out of the microwave and ate it all in three big bites. He washed it down with a cold bottle of water and as he guzzled it down, his phone rang.

"Chief Phill" He answered.

"I don't talk on phones. That's too impersonal. Where are you located and I'll come to you?" Patricia's voice was seductive, luring.

He gave her his work office address and waited for her to arrive. She lived only one hour away from there. He had thought she moved out of state, got as far as possible away from Neil by now. But maybe some people can only go as far as she got.

***

Patricia walked in and Chief Phill's mouth dropped. He didn't mean for it to happen, but she was quite a stunning woman. She wore a quarter sleeved black, v-neck shirt that was a little form fitted, a tight pair of jeans that teased men with the curves of her body, and her hair and makeup was done.

She had choppy black hair with straight across bangs and her red lipstick was bright and desirable. And she was still rocking the black liner cat eye look with those icy blue eyes. She sat down in the chair in front of his desk, crossed one leg over the other and slouched.

"So, what is it you need from me?" She looked him in the eyes until he looked away. She could tell this made him uncomfortable and her lips pursed up in a half smile at him.

"Well, first of all I want to thank you for coming all this way on such a short notice. Is there anything I can get you? Water? A cola?

135

We have a vending machine that I can get a snack out of for ya. My treat."

"I'll take a coke. Sure." she slid her chair up right at Chief Phill's desk.

He watched her do this. He was about to tell her that wasn't necessary, but saw her rest her elbows with her head sitting in her hands. He went to the staff room to grab her a coke.

When he walked back in his office, Patricia had switched positions. She was then standing and looking at his achievements hung on the walls.

"Smart man." She stood with her hands in her back pockets and looked tiny from his angle, fragile.

"Thank you. What do you do you for a living, Patricia?" he handed her the coke and thought about how his question sounded more like an interrogation, an accusation than a question.

She grabbed the coke from his hand and looked at him with disappointment. "What's it to you?"

"That's not why you're here. I'm not judging, I just wanted to break the ice. That's all."

Patricia sat back down in her designated seat. "I volunteer as a crisis hotline operator. I also live in a half-way house." She cracked open the can of coke and it hissed at her. She looked at him to see if she could find judgement his eyes. If he'd lean his body away from her like she had a deathly virus.

Chief Phill stayed in his position, he didn't judge her. How could he? He had one phone conversation with her mom and he knew she was raised in hell.

"Only the strongest of people can work at a crisis center. Thank you for your services."

She had the can of coke up to her mouth, like she was about to take a drink and stopped once she heard what he said. She gave him a blank look. "I don't need you to tell me I'm doing a good job, okay? Your approval means nothing to me. Get down to the nitty gritty. What the hell is it you want, Chief Phill?" She took that drink she was going for before she was interrupted, and gazed at him over the can she held in the air to her mouth.

"Neil, your ex-husband—"

"Just call him Neil. You can leave out the whole ex-husband part." She interrupted.

Chief Phill liked her attitude. She had confidence in there. He had underestimated her.

"Neil's current wife is missing and I'm hoping you can help me understand Neil a little better. I've spoken to Claudia and she said she found out about you later on, after they got married. That and upon many other reasons is why she divorced him."

"Okay" She took another gulp from the coke.

"What was Neil like to you? Towards you? How did he act?"

"Ha!" She covered her mouth and shook her head. "He was a nightmare. That's what he was. Is."

"What kinds of things would he do? Were you scared of him?"

"Yes. Actually, I was scared of him. I'd been in several abusive relationships before him, but he was a whole different breed."

"What did he do? Were you ever scared he might kill you?" He had hoped this question wouldn't push her to get up and leave.

"I *knew* he would've killed me. That's why I left him." She placed her arms on his desk and leaned in closer to him. She looked him in the eyes and he noticed how pretty they were.

Icy blue and seductive. He knew she wasn't trying to seduce him, though. It was just part of her, something she had learned at a young age around men. Then she said it.

"I would check every body of water, every forest out there you can find, any abandoned building. Check any place you can hide a body. She's not coming home alive if he had something to do with her disappearance. I can guarantee you, he did."

Chief Phill squinted his eyes at her and rocked and back forth in his chair. The thing he does when he's thinking hard. "Had he ever threatened to kill you?"

"Not with words. His eyes did." She leaned back in her seat. "Check all bodies of water first."

He shook his head and stood from his chair. "Looks like I've got some work to do."

"I hope she can get a proper burial and be put to rest." She grabbed her purse and crossed her arms.

"Take care of yourself, Patricia. I'll be in touch." he held out his hand to shake hers.

She kept her arms crossed, hesitated, then quickly and lightly shook his hand. She drew her hand back, fast and crossed her arms again.

# Present Day

"Think." Chief Phill sits in a hospital chair, with a notepad and pen ready to catch the prick who did this to her. "Let's start at the beginning."

Willow pushes the buttons on the side of the hospital bed, reclining forward and backward over and over. Looking straight ahead, she says nothing to him.

Hanging his head, he lets out a sigh. "Willow, you're not in trouble, okay? You're a victim of a crime." he pulls out a missing poster picture with her face on it and hands it to her. "Everyone's been looking for you. You've certainly been missed."

Willow shuffles in the hospital bed and sits up, taking the daydream she had for months out of his hands. In the picture she wears a big smile that shows her straight, white teeth.

Her blonde hair is down and one side is behind her ear. Her collar bones show and the charm necklace she always wears, glints from the flash of the camera. She's wearing a floral, red shirt and just a touch of makeup on her face. The picture is in color, so she feels important then.

*Mommy and daddy really do care.*

"When can I see my parents?" She handed him back the poster.

"I just need to ask you some questions first." the curves of Chief Phill's mouth are down.

"Can I get some rest first? This isn't exactly easy." she yawns a little.

"I understand. I'll be back." as he's walking out of her room he stops at the door and says. "Willow, this isn't your fault. Okay?" he looks at her, and pictures his own daughter laying in that bed.

She shakes her head in agreement and purses her lips together.

Willow leans back and reflects on the day she escaped Brock's imprisonment.

***

I had sex with him. And that's when he unlocked the chains and let me free, for a certain distance anyway. I wasn't allowed out of the house. No phones were within my vicinity to call for help.

He had changed the dead bolt lock so he could lock me in from the outside when he left. He boarded up every window before he unchained me. I watched him hammer my freedom of natural light away as I bit my nails and soaked up the last bit I would feel or see of the sun.

I had more room to roam then. I could watch T.V. but I couldn't use the internet because he had a password I could never figure out. He left knives out within my reach, and would watch my face as I'd gaze at them.

*His way of shackling me up again.*

I didn't have it in me to stab him anyway. The thought of blood pouring out of a body made my stomach churn. I think he knew that.

It was the sixty-eighth day, *I think,* according to my keeping time on the clocks. When he left for *'work'* which really meant when he left to buy more supplies to make that town home even more like a dungeon, using his daddy's money.

*Swipe, swipe, daddy. You created a monster.*

I searched around for weapons. This was my first time being alone there unshackled. Brock had locks on all the cabinets except one. That one was dedicated to me.

It was filled with Styrofoam bowls and plates, plastic wear and every kind of snack you could think of. All drawers were locked, too and I couldn't find anything I could use as a weapon. I didn't want to kill him. I just wanted to hurt him enough that he lay there for hours, giving me time to flee.

Brock got home holding brown paper grocery bags and began emptying them onto the counter. "Does spaghetti sound good for dinner?"

140

I shook my head, because *yes* it did sound good. My mouth watered.

He invited me to cook with him, and smiled at me while he chopped vegetables.

"Boil a pot of water for the noodles, would ya?"

And I did as I was told. I grabbed the biggest, tallest pot I could find and filled it to the brim and watched it simmer to a boil.

"Here" He turned the stove top down to low "Go ahead and put the noodles in there." Brock sat the box on the counter by where I stood.

Putting cooking mittens on my hands so I'm protected from the steam, I felt the softness against my skin and every sense was heightened right then. Except for my hearing.

But loud and clear I heard *Do it.* I placed all the noodles in the pot, turned the burner on high, and as it simmered to a boil over the brim, Brock was saying something to me and I turned to look at him.

He slowly walked towards me. I grabbed the pot of boiling noodle water and splashed every drop on his face. I watched his skin blister and slide off his face as he screamed in despair.

I grabbed the knife he cut vegetables with, just in case, and made a run for the front door. I was almost there and he grabbed me from behind, wrapping both his arms around, then slammed me on the floor and kicked my stomach repeatedly, as hard as he could, with his steel toe boots he wore daily to be in character of his dungeon building expertise.

I rolled into a ball and screamed in dread. Because the pain was excruciating. I could barely move and I felt a warm wetness between my legs. I reached down and touched the goo, then saw the blood as I held my hand up to see what made a puddle down there.

I saw him lying on the floor just ahead of me, and watched his chest pump up and down. He writhed in pain now that it fully kicked in. But he still thought he caught me again, so he rested as his skin boiled and slid off more.

I pulled my body up with both hands against the floor and saw blood forming even more between my legs. I grabbed a hold of my stomach and looked at Brock's face.

He looked damaged, weak, deformed, like a real monster. I thought he was sleeping now. I searched around and found the knife under the couch and grabbed it, and I wouldn't stab him unless he touched me again. I ran to the front door clasping the knife and my stomach, except this time I smelled smoke.

Inhaling the fumes had me wheezing and the heat from fire cinched my skin. I opened the front door and Neil shoved me behind it, without realizing I was right there. I listened to his feet bang against the floors as he called out for Brock.

"I'm gonna kill you, mother fucker!" He poured gasoline around the already lit areas.

*This was my chance.*

I dropped the knife and swiftly walked out from behind the door. The other side was within my reach. I was only a foot away from freedom. But I had to get something from Brock first.

Coughing and wheezing again, I felt around in each pocket of Brock's pants. He lay there, barely moving his head to watch me. His words were raspy and hard to hear. "I…. love…. you" he whimpered.

I had what I needed then and when I reached the line separating me and freedom, I practically crawled over it. I was doubled over, holding my stomach. Right before I shut the door, I saw Neil, and we locked eyes for a second.

His dark eyes almost lured me back into his arms. "Willow!" he shouted in that foreign accent of his.

*My knight in shining armor.*

But he wasn't really. He was a monster, just like Brock. They can both burn in the hell of that dungeon together. It was their turn for prison now. He called out to me over and over, and his legs galloped like ten steps in one. My heart pounded through my chest.

I slammed the door shut and used the key Brock always carried around in his pocket and locked them both in.

I'd like to say the house shoots up in flames and busts out the windows. But that's not how it really works. Fire ignited their flesh and haunting moans bellowed through the walls of that dungeon, finding its way to my ears.

I plugged them with my fingers and squinted my eyes closed tightly. My throat tightened and my mouth went dry. I screamed and my heart thudded against my ribcage, like a fish flopping in place of my heart.

The flames made a reflection in my eyes like fireworks. And still, nobody came outside. Brock was right; the old folks around here *really* can't hear. I didn't stay to witness the whole act, so I don't know if the windows bust out or the house shoots up in flames like they do in movies.

I backed away as the fire grew, and took off running, falling every few steps to the field where the deer live. My abdomen rushed blood down my legs even more and I stopped when I reached the distance nobody could see.

I spotted a bucket isolated behind a gathering of matured trees. It was heavy to pick up, but adrenaline rushed through me. The bucket was filled with earth worms and dirt. I dumped them in a bush and carried it to a spot far enough away they couldn't crawl on me. I turned the bucket upside down and sat on the bottom of it; finally, being able to catch my breath.

# Three Months Later

Today, I am free.
Free of Neil.
Free of Brock.
Free of motherhood.
*And,* I'm free from work.

Yes, they've given me paid leave. I got myself a new flat, decorated in shabby chic tapestries and colorful Moroccan knobs on every cabinet, drawer and door. It's so beautiful and so... me.

I'm so proud of it. It's an expensive flat, but I don't have to worry too much about being on time with rent every month. I'm the girl who survived a house fire by two men holding me captive, raping me and impregnating me, torturing me and forcing my abortion.

Case closed.

Plauen, who Neil referred to as my *nosey neighbor*, helped out in the case.

"I always felt like he'd hurt her. That man has a temper." she told the police. *Thank you, Pauleen.*

Mr. and Mrs. Grey, (the nice couple who saved me) come visit me every month. I like them. They sort of treat me like I'm their daughter. At least, I think this is how loving parents act.

They give me advice, support me in my endeavors and call me every week to check up on me. My parents, well, they're still who they are despite what all I've been through. I thought this would change something in them. I hoped they'd be more affectionate and involved in my life after realizing they could have never seen me again, but no.

So, I just love them from a distance. I'm learning to love myself better.

Claudia and Patricia reached out to me through Facebook, and now we keep in touch. They're glad Neil is dead. And so am I. We counsel each other from what all we endured from Neil. Claudia was never a drug addict. Neil lied. No surprise there.

Patricia had changed her last name and is extremely hard to find on social media or in any records if you're looking for the Patricia without her newest last name. I have finally found more friends, though.

A book is being written about my survival. Victim turned victor. People from all over the world send me letters and money. They ask me to sign the book for them when it's published. I'll do it. Whatever I can do to keep the money flowing in.

At the beach, the sand feels soft between my toes and I dig them in deeper and deeper into the soft white sand. It's a breezy day and the wind blows the sun hat off my head.

I stand up and sand covers my back side. I wipe it away as I jog after my hat. It dances in the air and drops to the ground, fumbling on its side and is stopped by a man's sandy foot. Him and I both reach for it, lock eyes and we laugh together. His eyes are as blue as the sky on this beautiful day.

*I can't do it again. I can't date. I have to focus on me.*

His hair is thick, just like I like it and he's tan, with a built body. He's wearing swim trunks that are wet from his swimming, and I can see what he's got packin'. I look away and place the hat back on my head and thank him for his help.

"You have a beautiful smile." is his response to that.

*Is that a foreign accent I hear?*

# Acknowledgements

It's time to thank all the people who worked zealously to bring this book into your hands. Everyone at Pen It! Publications, I thank you.

With the lovely team of cover designers, editors, marketers and the publishing, you've helped this book become a dream come true to me and I thank you even more so for putting up with the countless hours, emails, and texts back and forth about every little detail. Your patience is like no other!

A huge thank you to my husband, who listened to me read Willow's Flame out loud to him multiple times and showed excitement and support each time. He is my rock. I also thank my daughters for tip toeing through sometimes while I worked day and night on writing and rewriting, as well as showing just as much excitement and support for me as I do for them with their endeavors. They are the best daughters a mother could ever ask for.

To my twin brother, earth parents, and friends- You all helped me so much throughout this journey of Willow's Flame. Thank you for picking up my phone calls to ask, "Do you think this sounds good?" and answering honestly. And I thank you for clapping and cheering me on through social media, as well.

Another huge shout-out goes to all of my readers for believing in my book and for your honest and lovely feedback.

Finally, I raise a glass to all the Authors out there who inspired me with your own words of wisdom and praise.

Author Stephanie Fields is a fiction suspense writer and reader. She likes to be surprised when she reads, and she loves to give the same shock value to her readers. Her writing has been featured Internationally on Margate Bookie Zine as well as published on all e-Book outlets.

She lives in Texas with her husband, two daughters, dog and several chickens that she names after book characters.

She graduated in 2016 from A&M with a Bachelor's Degree and is currently pursuing a Master's Degree in Forensic Psychology because that is her all-time favorite subject to study.

**Read on for an excerpt from Stephanie Fields' novel,**
*I Am Rotten*

**Coming to shelves in 2022**

I am rotten
Rotten to the core
I am not the one you're searching for
Damaged, scarred inside and out
Mysteriously, you wonder what I am about
Don't push that button
Remember, I am rotten
I am rotten to the core
I'll leave you wanting the life you had before
-Beth

# That Night

Shawn shuffled his legs back and forth and anxiously hopped up and down. His heart felt like it would eventually pound right out of his chest and plop down on the ground.

"Come on, man. Hurry up!" He held both hands in his letter man jacket pockets, clinching his class ring in his hand so tightly that it left indentations from his graduation year numbers and the mascot's face on his palm. He ducked when a car drove by.

Tying the ropes in double knots, "Shut *up*, dude! I'm trying! Can't you see?!" Clint spouted with heavy breathing.

The interstate bridge was never busy at three in the morning. The small town of Jefferson in Texas sleeps off the midnight murders. Nothing good can happen with two teenage boys out past ten at night.

"Got it." Clint panted and peeved, doubled over with his hands on his knees. "Now help me dump it over"

"What? No. Fuck that." Shawn held up his hands in the air and backed away. "I'm the onlooker. Remember?"

"Shawn! I can't pick this up by myself!"

"Shit, dude." Tears sprang to Shawn's eyes, and he wiped them away with the back of his hand. "I can't." His chin quivered up and down, "I can't do it."

"Here, put these on." Clint handed him gloves he pulled out of his jean pocket, and Shawn noticed the white ones he wore were ripped, showing a little of his hands raw and pink from the rope tying with a smudge of their victim's blood on his pointer finger.

Shawn grabbed the gloves and put them on, then paced back and forth in front of his car. They kept the headlights off and covered his license plate with duct tape just in case anyone has a damn good memory.

"Look at me." Clint grabbed Shawn's face with both of his hands and gripped tightly. "Look at me right now. Nobody is going to find out shit. We get this done quickly and get it done together. Got it?"

Shawn glanced down and started crying a little bit. "Stop being such a pussy! Man the fuck up!" He placed his hand under Shawn's chin and lifted it up to be eye to eye. "This is your car. You want this shit on your hands?" Shawn shook his head no. "Then fucking help me before someone sees us!"

Clint and Shawn picked up the body wrapped in an old blanket with ropes tied around the body's neck, stomach and ankles as blood seeped through and left stains behind on their shirts. They struggled with the dead weight. The body felt more heavy dead than it did alive. They weren't expecting the task of getting the corpse over the side of the bridge to be *this* difficult. And with both of their strength together, they pushed the body over.

They watched as their victim dove straight into the deep blue *and soon to be red*. They heard a big splash and witnessed the form sink to the bottom of its new home.

Made in the USA
Columbia, SC
05 June 2022